THE TIPPLE TWINS AND THE GIFT

THE TIPPLE TWINS
AND
THE GIFT

If you were being tormented
would you run… or stand and fight?

Michelle Cordara

This is a work of fiction. Names, characters, businesses, places, events
and incidents are either the products of the author's imagination
or used in a fictitious manner. Any resemblance to actual persons,
living or dead, or actual events is purely coincidental.

Matador
9 Priory Business Park,
Wistow Road, Kibworth Beauchamp,
Leicestershire. LE8 0RX
Tel: 0116 279 2299
Email: books@troubador.co.uk
Web: www.troubador.co.uk/matador
Twitter: @matadorbooks

ISBN 978 1800460 317

British Library Cataloguing in Publication Data.
A catalogue record for this book is available from the British Library.

Printed and bound in Great Britain by 4edge Limited
Typeset in 11pt Baskerville by Troubador Publishing Ltd, Leicester, UK

For Kane, Jessica, Sienna, Bobbi, Tristan and Roman.

A BIT ABOUT TWINS...

Identical twins always look the same, apart from a few minor details, like moles, scars, birthmarks, etc. One might have a squint in their eyes, the other may have a tooth that sticks out, or one may even have longer hair than the other. Either way, these are only very tiny details, and irrespective of this, identical twins are very hard to tell apart.

Identical twins sometimes sound the same, so be sure which one you're speaking to on the phone when sharing all your deepest and darkest secrets.

Identical twins have a very special bond that can make a lot of people envious, and no one really understands it.

Some identical twins are even known to have made up their own special language so that none of their family or friends can understand what they're saying and they just live in their very own identical twin world.

Identical twins are special, and, if you're an identical twin, consider yourself to be very lucky indeed! Unless...

CHAPTER ONE

*

NO MAGIC ALLOWED!

Jenna and Jessica Tipple were identical twins. But not *ordinary* identical twins.

Jenna and Jessica were eight years old and lived at 157 Bacton Square in London. You could spot their house a mile away because it was the only house on the square with blackbirds perched on the roof and the steps outside the front door. Many of the neighbours thought this was very peculiar and so they avoided the Tipples at all costs. According to Mrs Griffins, London was dirty enough as it was without them attracting *more* wildlife. Mrs Griffins was an old woman who lived two doors down from the Tipples, and her opinions stretched as long as her fingers did. Mrs Tipple said Mrs Griffins' fingers were long so she could dig around in everyone's business and her nails were forever black because of all the dirty secrets she knew about everyone. Jenna and Jessica had seen these black nails once, and between them they decided she saved the dirt for her special occasion dinners.

The Wilsons, who lived between the Tipples and Mrs Griffins, weren't any better. They were the most boring couple on the square and hadn't had any children because they couldn't do with disruption and interference in their boring routines. Mrs Griffins and Mr and Mrs Wilson would have lengthy conversations over the black railings between the houses that would consist of nothing more than what colour socks they were wearing or how warm they liked to have their bath water. When Mrs Griffins approached the matter of the blackbirds on the Tipples' house, Mr Wilson would simply shrug and say, 'I don't know.' This was something far too abnormal and outrageous for the Wilsons to think about. They disliked eccentric people.

Of the Tipples, Mrs Tipple was the most uncomfortable about their odd ways. She would be forever throwing bird seed outside and screaming, 'God, I love nature!' at the top of her lungs to make it look like she wanted the blackbirds there and that it wasn't because the Tipples attracted strange things like this.

But this wasn't the worst of it, not by a long way. The Tipples had a secret 'pet' who slept under the twins' beds at night. This pet was called Boo… and Boo was a ghost. Boo was a very young ghost who looked like a typical ghost, if a child was to describe one. Boo was like a fat, round white blanket with dark circles for eyes and chubby stumpy arms sticking out from his sides.

Boo didn't like leaving the house alone, or very often at all, but he did like hiding in dark corners and occasionally reading bedtime stories to the twins. Boo was very shy, and on occasion they would put him in a pram at night and take him for walks, which Boo appreciated immensely. He would point and laugh at the trees and birds as if he'd never seen such things before.

He told the twins he had found his forever home with them, because before the Tipples, when other families had lived in 157 Bacton Square, Boo would poke his head out of whatever shadow he was hiding in and say 'Hello' and whoever was living there moved out within a week. It was only on the day that the Tipples moved in that things changed for the better.

It was six years ago and on a grey Saturday morning in mid-March. Boo had been hiding in a dark corner in the kitchen when he heard a van park outside in the square. He'd heard the voices of little girls and the sound of their feet as they exited the vehicle.

'Come this way,' he'd heard an older voice say. A woman's voice. A mother's voice.

He'd heard the unlocking of the front door echoing around the empty house before hearing the scampering of tiny feet running through the living room.

'Potty, Mummy!' said an innocent voice.

'Quick, upstairs, Jenna. The potty's in the van. Get to the toilet!'

'Potty, Mummy!' said a different voice.

'Oh, Jessica, quickly. You upstairs as well – follow Jenna.'

Boo heard the little ones rushing up the stairs before seeing another little girl with long, thick honey-coloured hair hovering around in the dining room holding a cuddly brown bear. Boo edged out a little.

'What do you think of the house then, Caitlyn?' said a man's voice. A dad's voice. Boo could see this man. He was tall with dark hair and he was struggling with some heavy boxes.

'I think this house is big,' said the little girl, 'but not too big. Does Jamie have his own bed?' she said, squeezing her teddy bear.

Mr Tipple looked at the brown bear in the girl's arms and said, 'Jamie can share your bed, because that's what cuddly bears are for,' and the little girl smiled.

Boo looked down at his hands. They were empty. Boo didn't have a cuddly bear like the little girl. Boo felt a bit lonely.

Moments later, Mrs Tipple came down the stairs with the other two children. Boo could see they were younger than the little girl called Caitlyn.

'We need a change of clothes' said Mrs Tipple, peeping in some boxes. Mrs Tipple had blonde hair. She looked friendly. 'Jenna went to the toilet but Jessica didn't quite make it,' she said.

'That's terrible twos for you,' said Mr Tipple, sweeping the girl known as Jessica into his arms. Jessica hugged her dad back.

Boo couldn't remember the last time he'd been hugged like that, and he found himself hugging his little round white body. Boo then moved a little closer. He wanted to see more of this family and crept further into the light. The three little girls were running around while their mum and dad unpacked.

Boo wanted to say hello but couldn't. Not now he'd seen how the family was. He'd seen this many times. They were a close family. He'd been turned down by these sort of people before. Just one look at him and they ran a mile. Boo thought it was best to stay hidden. He turned his back, but then something magical happened.

'Hello,' said a voice.

Boo turned to see Caitlyn staring straight at him.

'What's your name?' she said boldly.

'My name?' said Boo.

'Yes, your name.'

'I haven't been asked that question in a long time. I can't remember how to answer it,' said Boo shyly.

'Shall I start?' said Caitlyn, kneeling down.

'Yes please,' said Boo.

'My name is Caitlyn. I am four years old.'

'And my name's Boo!' said Boo excitedly. 'And I think I am five.'

'That's a funny name,' said Caitlyn back. 'A funny name for a funny-looking boy. Mummy! Look, Mummy, we have a friend! We have a funny-looking friend. Isn't he funny, Mummy?'

'Oh,' said Mrs Tipple, walking into the kitchen with the two little ones scampering by her feet. Seeing Boo's ghostly presence, she paused.

'His name is Boo, Mummy.'

'Oh,' said Mrs Tipple again. 'I wasn't expecting a… Are you on your own, Boo?'

Boo nodded.

'Doesn't he look funny, Mummy?'

'Yes, yes he does. You are funny-looking, Boo. But you are *perfectly* funny.'

Boo smiled. Relieved.

'Boo said he is five, but if he is five, where is his mummy and daddy?' asked Caitlyn.

'Well maybe Boo doesn't have a mummy or a daddy. Boo, do you have parents?'

Boo had to think about this one. He remembered having parents once upon a time. But that's where the problem was. It was 'once upon a time'.

'I used to,' Boo said

'And where are they now?' said Mrs Tipple softly.

'I think they are where I should have gone,' said Boo.

'And where's that?'

'Heaven. Do you know where it is?'

'I know about it, Boo, but I can't take you there. Did you all try to get there together?'

'No. I went first, but my mum...' Boo stopped when he noticed the dad had now made an appearance. Mr Tipple gave Boo a warm smile, which encouraged Boo to carry on. 'I went first but my mum and dad didn't come with me,' he said finally.

'Is that why you stayed?'

'Yes. I used to look like you. I had blonde hair but my eyes were blue. Only I got very poorly. I was sick in bed and then one night I closed my eyes.'

'And then what?' said Mrs Tipple, now crossing her legs on the cold kitchen floor with Jenna and Jessica sucking their thumbs either side of her.

'Well, I wanted to close my eyes but my mum was crying for me to not close them, but I couldn't help it. They were so heavy and I was so cold I had to shut them.' Boo stopped. Boo couldn't tell them this. It was going to come out wrong. Sound stupid. They had listened up until now but surely not for much longer.

'Carry on,' said Mrs Tipple, nodding.

'Well, when I did I wasn't in my bed any more. I was in the air. And something was telling me to float higher and higher. It wasn't a voice though – more a feeling. But I couldn't leave my mum and dad. I could see them looking over me on my bed.'

'And then what did you do, Boo?'

'I floated down to them. My mum was telling my old body in my bed that she loved me and that she would miss me. She was cuddling me and crying on me. My dad was holding her shoulders and he was crying too. I'd never seen my parents cry before. I wanted them to know they didn't have to miss me. They didn't have to cry any more. So I stayed by them and cuddled them, but they didn't cuddle me back. I spoke to them to let them know I was there but they didn't hear me. I stayed for days, weeks, and even more days. How many days do you have to add up to get to today?'

'I don't know, Boo. I don't know how long ago it was.'

'It was a very long time ago.'

'And when was the last time you saw your mum and dad, Boo?' said Mr Tipple.

'I remember them talking about moving out. It was because of me. It was because they couldn't look at these walls any more without me being there. Why couldn't they see me but other people can?'

'I don't know, Boo. Maybe because they have memories of what you used to look like and maybe that's the way it's meant to stay,' said Mrs Tipple.

'I remember the day they left. I was the one that was crying then. They had lots of bags and other things. They even had my toys. And they just left. Forever. I looked out of the window and watched them go. I was scared, because who was going to look after me?'

'Could you not follow them, Boo?'

'No, I can't. I can't leave here. I don't know why. It's fear that holds me back, I think.'

'And what makes you think your parents are in heaven now?'

'I get feelings. It's hard to explain. For example, I look at you all and I can feel something strong. I don't know what it is. But it's there. And that's what it was like for me when I woke up one morning and felt something about my mum and dad. I just knew they were gone. First of all it was my dad. And then, a lot of days after, it was my mum.'

'Well, Boo, let me tell you something. You aren't on your own any more. We will look after you.'

'I know I won't be with you forever. I think I need looking after first. I think I need to go the way I was meant to go before.'

'Boo, if you need to go again that's okay. Everybody goes at some point or another. And when it's your time to go again, don't hold back for us. You go and you float up high. You keep floating as much as you need to. And you know what?'

'What?' said Boo.

'I think when you do you will find your mum and dad again.'

And that is how the Tipples met Boo.

Boo was five years old, but in death he was more than that. And this showed. He was very childlike in play and in the way he understood things. However, he was very wise at times. It was as if he had an intuition only an elderly person would have. Or should we say a *ghost*. But this was okay for the Tipples. It was just another odd thing to rack up on their list. And for Boo, he discovered a great way to overcome his fear of leaving the house, and that was friendship. Because without the Tipples encouragement, he never would have left those walls ever again.

*

Because of all the strange nonsense the Tipples had surrounding them, you would probably think that Jenna and Jessica were used to strange looks and whispering behind their backs, but truthfully, they didn't ever get used to it at all. They never really knew whether they were coming or going, because if the neighbours in Bacton Square weren't shutting blinds or closing doors whenever the Tipples passed, the public would be pointing or staring at the twins, because they were the only identical twins in the whole of England. For some strange reason, every twin, every identical twin, had vanished from the face of the earth. Except for Jenna and Jessica Tipple that is, and nobody knew why.

Mrs Tipple told the girls they were special, and that they must take great care of themselves if they're ever left on their own. Although they felt overwhelmed at the thought of people thinking they were special, Jenna and Jessica Tipple *hugely* disagreed with finger-pointing. It was very rude in their book. It was a strict rule in the Tipple house and one that had to be obeyed at all times. After all, you never knew what strange things might happen if you were to point your fingers at others.

In Jenna's and Jessica's experience, by accident of course, they had made someone throw up alphabet spaghetti and made them say the alphabet backwards all at the same time. To most children this would be seen as very amusing, but not to the Tipple twins. It was most inappropriate and something they had to learn to control, especially when in public.

'Others just don't warm to gifted people like us!' Mrs Tipple would say on one of her rants. She ranted so much about finger-pointing that whenever she was on the subject her speech got faster and faster and her voice got more and more high pitched so that she sounded like she'd taken too much helium. 'We must *try* to act *normal*!' was what she said most frequently, and everyone knew that when she used the word 'gifted' she really meant 'magic' and when she used the word 'normal' she really meant 'no magic allowed!'

But '*normal*' proved to be harder in some cases than others. The Tipples couldn't help the doors occasionally opening on their own when entering the house or another room, and they definitely couldn't help it when the doors decided to slam on people's faces (if it was someone they didn't like on the other side of it).

Trying to pretend to be 'normal' wasn't easy. It meant pretending to be somebody you're not, which was the hardest thing the Tipple twins ever had to do. It was like locking a tiger up and telling it to live like a mouse. But no matter how hard it was, the Tipple twins had no interest in finding out what would happen to them if they were ever unsuccessful. Pretending to be somebody you're not was – in their eyes – their only option.

CHAPTER TWO

*

THE FLOATING WOMAN

It was a Saturday morning, and the twins had the rarity of waking up without Billy Buck shouting out and throwing stones at the windows.

Billy Buck was a boy who was the same age as the twins who lived around the corner and gave them endless amounts of grief for being 'different'. The twins found it hard to ignore, especially as he had a huge front tooth that seemed to take centre stage of his whole face like it was running for president.

The twins took their time to put their dressing gowns on (ignoring the blackbirds that began lining up on the windowsill outside) and opened their bedroom door together. They didn't notice the raindrops beginning to fall, even though there were no clouds in sight, nor did they notice a blackbird sitting on the chest of drawers shaking raindrops off its feathers.

Mornings were the hardest part of the day for the twins, as they had to relive the reality that they no longer had an older sister. Caitlyn had been gone for two years now, and no matter what anyone said to them, nothing made them feel any better about it.

Lucy Loop, at Gospel Glums School, had a habit of passing on stories about how much of a horror her five older brothers were, and that the twins had had a lucky escape.

Unfortunately for the twins, Lucy Loop was their only friend (if you could call her that). Jenna and Jessica found it a difficult task when it came to making friends. They mainly spent the day isolating themselves from the crowd, as they had learned that people were too quick to judge. With their rare double-act appearance and awkward social skills, no child wanted to be seen hanging around with the Tipple twins. It was only Lucy Loop, the class gossip, who seemed eager to interrogate the twins into spilling stories of their private life, which the twins decided to ignore at all costs – unless they were stuck with her during teamwork exercises. That couldn't be helped.

What made it worse was the fact that Lucy Loop had a never-ending runny nose, and if weren't runny, it was crusty on the edges of her nostrils. It was the twins' priority during the school day to avoid sitting next to her at lunchtime. And if they ever did, it would result in the pair of them heaving and gagging and not eating any lunch at all. This always got them into trouble at home if their mum found out. She clearly didn't care about bogies.

Jenna and Jessica had little interest in their appetites since Caitlyn's disappearance, but they made the journey downstairs for breakfast all the same. Squinting as they walked past what was once their older sister's bedroom (to avoid looking at it), they bumped into each other as a result, which made a somewhat easy journey into a more difficult one. Finally reaching the hallway downstairs, with their honey-coloured hair almost tangled up in each other's, they pretended they never noticed Caitlyn's shoes, left by the front door *exactly* where she'd last took them off.

Picking up the morning paper together, they found themselves removing feathers off it, which they'd never had to do before. But they read it all the same and saw that their sister Caitlyn had taken up the front page news again. A name that remains in the papers still to this day. A name that is constantly dragged up by the public and by the media because nobody can let this case go. A case that has been open for two years and remains open because Caitlyn Tipple is not a twin, and people can't understand why she has been taken by the black figure when she clearly isn't a double. As they stood and read together, they saw that the headline said: 'CAITLYN TIPPLE STILL MISSING … THE FIRST PERSON TO DISAPPEAR THAT WASN'T A TWIN.' They continued reading the article unenthusiastically. They knew that if this had landed inside their door … it had also landed inside many others. Jenna and Jessica felt their cheeks turn a little pink.

As they read, they saw that PC Dilks, the officer in charge of the investigation (and well-known mummy's boy), had been interviewed and said:

'Even though there had been no significant events in her personal life leading up to Caitlyn's disappearance, there is strong evidence that links this case to the missing twins all over the country, as there have been sightings of a black figure, possibly a woman, who was seen moments before Caitlyn vanished.' The reporter then asked what the public should do if they see the black figure, to which PC Dilks replied, 'The public need to remain calm and dial 999 immediately, but please be sure as to what you have seen. In the past we have had people phoning in reporting black dogs and cats. Someone even reported the shadow of a lamp post.'

When the reporter asked Dilks about the rumour that when he was off-duty one night at home he called 999 reporting a black figure that turned out to be his coat hanging up by the front door, he replied, 'No comment.'

The reporter then said that a homeowner and stamp collector had been quoted as saying: 'Actually, I turned all the lights off in my house to make sure I didn't mistake any shadows for anything … Well, it wasn't very good because I was in complete darkness and thought I had already been snatched by the black figure.'

PC Dilks then admitted that, because it's summer, he hasn't received a lot of calls regarding this case as people are less afraid of the dark. In fact, the most important thing he'd received this week was a candy crush request – from his mum.

The paper had used the same photo they'd always used of Caitlyn. It was her Gospel Glums School photo. Little did the Tipples know that when this school photo was taken it was to be her last.

Before they entered the messy kitchen, Jenna held back a little and refused to move until she'd counted to ten in her head, a habit she'd picked up since Caitlyn had gone. Jenna felt a strong urge to do this, and by not doing so, she felt the Tipples could experience bad luck. Mrs Tipple was convinced it was due to her feeling the need to control a situation.

'Right, come on then,' she said once the counting had finished. Jessica had been waiting patiently by her side, longing for a day where she didn't have to wait for counting, knocking on tabletops or, Jenna's favourite, finger flicking. It was a risky habit, given the finger-pointing rule, but Jenna was adamant about continuing the odd behaviour.

When they entered the kitchen, their mum was standing by the window, as she did most mornings, with her spoon in her teacup, which was stirring the drink on its own. It wasn't until she looked up and noticed the paper and its contents that she became startled and grabbed it and made a dash for the phone. She began talking before she had even dialled.

'Hello? … Hello, Maud? … Maud? … *Maud?* … Is a-n-y-b-o-d-y t-h-e-r-e! … MAUD? … MAUD!' She continued her one-sided conversation with what she thought was her sister, Aunt Maud Boggins, and she cried to nobody about how she wished the papers would stop reminding her of the terrible event from two years ago and how the police had told the family to prepare for the worst if Caitlyn was ever found.

Eating as little cereal as they could get away with, the twins concentrated on the spoon still stirring inside the cup, which was now on the table in front of them.

No longer hearing their mum sobbing over the phone, they were reminded by the sight of the self-stirring spoon of a story she had told them years ago. It was one that had stuck with them ever since and was the main reason why they weren't allowed to use their magic. It was the story of 'The Floating Woman'. Mrs Tipple had once explained to the twins that getting caught making magic could cause great outrage and lead to severe punishments.

'Like what, Mum?' the girls asked on a cloudy Sunday nearly three years before.

'Never you mind. All you need to know is that the world can be full of horrid things, and the punishments for having an extraordinary gift are just some of those things,' she said, placing some biscuits and milk on the table, with Caitlyn, Boo, Jenna and Jessica all huddled on the floor wrapped in blankets by their mum's feet.

'Please, Mum, we won't tell anyone. We promise to keep it secret,' Caitlyn pleaded while brushing her hair away from her face with her fingers before stuffing a chocolate bourbon in her mouth.

'Okay, I'll tell you just one story. But you must promise to keep it secret and to never tell a soul.'

'We promise.'

'Not even Lucy Loop, your friend at school?'

'Not even Lucy Loop,' said Jenna and Jessica.

'Okay, sit closely then,' Mrs Tipple said, as she got up to turn off all the lights and reached for a torch to hand to them. 'You can never tell who's earwigging through walls… or peering through cracks,' she said, as she closed the curtains in the living room and wrapped all four of

them in more blankets. She sat in her chair in front of them and leaned forward so her face was close to theirs…
'And so the story goes like this…'

'Ah, I'm scared… I don't like it…'

'Boo,' Mrs Tipple said gently, 'I haven't started.'

'Oh, okay,' Boo said, settling back in the blankets, with Caitlyn, Jenna and Jessica giggling quietly.

'*Burrp!*'

'I don't know which one of you did that, but I'm going to pretend I didn't hear it,' said Mrs Tipple, waiting for the laughing to stop before carrying on. 'Right… once there was a woman who lived in a house at the top of an isolated hill, where only the postman would visit, and maybe the milkman in the mornings.'

'Yes…' the four of them said together eagerly.

'And she was happy living there, very happy, until children started playing stupid games outside her door.'

'Mum, we thought you said it was isolated.' Said Jenna.

'It was. But this is why it made her unhappy. She liked the peace and quiet. She didn't want rude children playing loudly outside her front door.'

'Mum?'

'Yes, Jessica.'

'Do you think we are rude when we play?'

'No, Jessica, but the point I'm trying to make is that the woman didn't like children playing outside her home. So one day she told them to clear off and go and play somewhere else.'

'That's not too bad.'

'Jenna, I haven't finished. A few days after she told them to go away, they came back and played even louder than before. Then the next day they came back and were louder and louder. They even started knocking on her door and running away.'

'Aah, we feel sorry for her,' said the twins. 'How old was she? What did she look like? Was she pretty? I bet she was…'

'Boo, shhh, let me finish. And girls, don't laugh at him,' Mrs Tipple said as she rolled up her sleeves before continuing. 'One night, the group of children came and played outside her door in the hope that it would stop her from sleeping, because she worked hard and sometimes liked early nights. And it did. It stopped her from sleeping. And do you know what it feels like for a hardworking adult to lose sleep due to careless children?'

'No.' They all said together.

'It can make a person very angry.'

'I'm scared,' Jessica said

'I'm even scareder,' Boo said, shivering.

'That's not even a *word*,' Caitlyn said, and they all laughed.

'Good. I'm glad you're scared,' Mrs Tipple butted in quickly, 'because she got so angry she cast a spell on all the children and turned them into ants.'

'Yuk! We would never use our magic for something horrible like that.'

'Good, I'm glad, but then the ants made their way into her home and ate all the food in her kitchen – even her home-made chocolate cake that she made every Sunday afternoon.'

'Uhh! That's just unforgivable,' Jenna said, disgusted.

'I don't think I'd mind too much,' Boo said. And the girls laughed some more.

'Please be quiet, girls. So, anyway, she had to turn them back into children. And when the children went home they told their parents what had happened. One child even claimed they were ill and that it was the woman who had made them ill.'

'What did their parents say?'

'They didn't believe them at first, but one parent went and spied on the house for a whole week and caught her making spells in her home.'

'What sort of spells?' Caitlyn asked, her big brown eyes widening behind her blanket.

'Only simple ones, like to help her cook dinner, or to turn on the TV. Which is understandable. I wouldn't mind being able to do that every now and then. But anyway, she got arrested for it and was taken to a circus, where she was made to dance in the air and had to stay there for the rest of her life, for the public to look at her and laugh.'

'Being made to dance in the air isn't too bad.'

'Oh, but it is, Jessica. It was the worst punishment you could get back then. And still is today. No one ever wants to be made to dance in the air.'

'We don't like this story,' Caitlyn said. 'And I can tell Jenna and Jessica don't like it either because I've barely got any blanket left.'

'What does Caitlyn know? She's the one moaning she has no blanket left,' huffed Jenna.

'Jenna and Jessica, give your sister her blanket back…
and I'm glad to hear it. It means you'll be extra careful
and not practise any magic in public.'

'We won't ever, we promise.'

And that is what they did. Kept their promise. They
also made sure they never told anyone about the story
itself. Apart from *one* time, just *once*, when Billy Buck tried
blocking the twins' path to their home with his friends.
They told him if he listened closely he would hear the
cry of the floating woman at night and she would come
and dance in his room when he was asleep. But as much
as Billy Buck trembled and chattered his big tooth against
the rest, he eventually said that he didn't care. Even his
mate next to him said that the story was 'well wet'. But the
tear in his eye and the lump in his throat told the Tipple
twins something different.

CHAPTER THREE

*

MAGIC MOODS

It was around four thirty in the afternoon when Jenna and Jessica entered the living room to hear their dad tell their mum he had just seen Mrs Griffins run outside her house with her arms flapping and yelling for someone to save her because she was just about to get killed by one of the blackbirds. Apparently, she flapped so much she nearly took off with one of them.

Mrs Tipple said it was ridiculous, because it was only last week she accused a bird of getting into her car and said it tried to drive off. And a month before that one had got into her bed with her slippers on and poured itself a cocoa.

When Jenna and Jessica looked out of the window they saw a shoe they guessed Mrs Griffins had left behind in the road, but above all things, they noticed the weather had changed and it looked like it was the beginning of a storm.

As dark clouds were now forming and a few raindrops were falling, people were putting up umbrellas, but they seemed to be struggling to keep hold of them. The Tipple twins ignored the blackbirds that were slowly gathering outside the window.

A little later that afternoon, Billy Buck shouted up to the twins' bedroom window for them to open it (causing Boo, who had just been floating in circles trying to catch his tail, to rush behind the curtain quivering with fright). And when they did, Billy Buck stood there with another boy, whose arms and face were covered in second class stamps (because he said he was going to post himself to America to visit his uncle there). They suggested to the twins to do the same thing, as London could do without rats.

'It takes one to know one!' shouted Jenna. She wished she could have thought of a better comeback than that one, but she had to say something quickly. She didn't trust Jessica to say the right thing. Nobody trusted Jessica to say the right thing. Jessica tripped up over words as easily as she did her own shadow. That was never good. Jessica disagreed with that slightly and felt she was never given a chance. But that's the price you have to pay for being the baby of the litter. The last one out. The runt.

There was an awkward stand-off between Jenna, Jessica and Billy Buck. They stared silently at one another. No one knowing what to do or say next. That was when they noticed there were more blackbirds than usual around the Tipples' home. One by one they were landing, not only on the house but all around the square. And there was a brave one that landed on Mrs Griffins' front door step.

Hearing their mum and dad rushing around in a panic downstairs, they closed their bedroom window and went to investigate to see what the noise was all about, shutting Boo in the wardrobe before doing so, as that was his safe place. As they entered the living room, their dad was standing hunched in the fireplace blocking what seemed to be blackbirds falling down the chimney.

'B-blasted birds!' Mr Tipple shouted. He was covered in soot and looked like a blackbird himself.

'I just don't understand what's going on. Why are they all here? Why so many?' Mrs Tipple said. 'We're going to have to blame this one on next door. We'll just say they copied us.' She then paused and looked at Caitlyn's shoes by the front door. 'No wonder we're the talk of the square.'

With Jenna and Jessica still fixated on the blackbirds outside (that continued to land in their hundreds), Billy Buck and his friend were now dancing in front of a group of birds, and when the birds tried to attack Billy's friend and his stamps, they ran off in a panic and told the birds to 'stay swag'.

But then the twins saw something emerge from the heavy rain … something that haunted them at night when they closed their eyes. Something that brought back bad memories of the night Caitlyn had gone. The twins covered their eyes with their hands, peering through the cracks of their fingers, to hide from the image that was scaring them. Three figures were coming towards their home.

With their dad still stuck in the chimney and their mum now writing a note to one of the neighbours to say 'We know you are copying us – please stop', the twins could see the figures getting closer and closer to the house. The twins weren't able to breathe or move, and a magical force from the twins made the doors lock, curtains close and the sofas slam against the living room door.

'For goodness' sake, girls, control your magic moods!' Mrs Tipple said, now scurrying towards the sofas with the note clutched tightly in her hand.

Mr Tipple got out of the fireplace to help her with the rearranged furniture, and birds were now flying around the living room. Mrs Tipple got the worst of it as they clawed at her hair.

'Oh, I've lost my note! My note to next door!'

With everyone waving their arms about to shoo the birds away, the twins eventually drew back the curtains and opened a window to let some of them out. It was then that they saw the figures getting even closer, making it clear to the girls who they actually were.

It was Aunt Maud and Uncle Patrick Boggins with Cousin Beatrice. They were breezing through the birds like they were elegantly crowdsurfing them.

There was a knock at the door.

'If that's a neighbour wanting to complain about the birds…!' Mr Tipple said, wiping off as much soot as he could from his face as he climbed over a sofa and opened the front door. 'Ah, it *all* makes sense now, the extra birds… the *weather*,' he said, disappointed.

Aunt Maud was wearing her usual green hat, slightly to one side, and Uncle Patrick still had no hair. They stood in the doorway with Cousin Beatrice between them. They should have known this really. Cousin Beatrice normally carried a dark cloud over her. She seemed to have that effect on people and the weather. Mrs Tipple had told Jenna and Jessica it was because she was one of those girls who just can't behave themselves, and because magic moods leak from the skin, the weather picks up on it if it's strong enough.

Jenna and Jessica never got on with Cousin Beatrice. She was two years older than them, the same age as their older sister Caitlyn, in fact, and she was the most spoilt girl in England. She was their 'cousinless cousin' because she quite simply denied the fact the Tipple twins were her relatives.

The Tipple twins hated everything about her. They hated her red hair, her freckles… Their mum told them it was a sign of beauty, but something told the twins they were a sign of something quite the opposite.

Beatrice was naturally plump but Aunt Maud would zap her with her fingers to make her skinny so Beatrice could afford to eat as much as she wanted without the doctors mentioning obesity.

'Well, are you going to let us in? Or are we going to stand out here in the rain? And honestly… you really do need to do something about those birds!' Aunt Maud said as she let her umbrella down. Knowing Aunt Maud, it was probably the most expensive umbrella you could buy.

Aunt Maud and Uncle Patrick Boggins had a lot of money. They had a habit of using their magic gift to change their lottery ticket numbers to the winning ones. Mr and Mrs Tipple deeply disapproved of this – no wonder Cousin Beatrice had been caught using her magic before. It's not like they ever set a good example. So, because they had money on tap, Aunt Maud and Patrick Boggins didn't work. Aunt Maud spent all day at home in her mansion attending to her ten cats and pruning her flowers, if that, while Uncle Patrick spent the day on his podgy bum reading newspapers and moaning about the bad weather.

'So sorry, come in. Tell your mother to put the kettle on. I'm sure she'll be pleased to see her sister,' Mr Tipple said with a false smile.

Aunt Maud tried lifting a podgy leg over one side of the sofa and she got stuck because her skirt wouldn't allow her to lift the other. She told Uncle Patrick she would have to spend the rest of the week in bed to get over the trauma and that he should check that no damage had been done to her designer boots. Uncle Patrick then did a dainty roll over the sofa so not to ruin his tailored suit, and landed softly on his bottom. Beatrice was skinny enough to fit through the gap and slid through unnoticed.

Mrs Tipple came back in from the kitchen with scratches on her face and tangled hair. Holding a tray of teacups, milk, sugar, a pot of tea and some cookies, she trod carefully over the remaining birds that were scattered on the floor. She murmured the words 'note … neighbours … lost … b-but' a few times before coming to her senses.

Aunt Maud said she needed at least ten sugars in her tea to help her with her own state of shock and put in well over twenty. 'Honestly, Sister,' she added, 'I know you've let things slip since Caitlyn's disappearance, but the state of this house is something else. You have to let her go. There's one thing wanting something you *need* and then there's just being plain greedy. You still have two daughters left!'

Aunt Maud then went on to insult Mr Tipple about his hygiene. 'You need to wash more regularly. Have you *seen* how dirty your skin is?' It was after this that the real topic of conversation, which everyone was waiting for, was raised, although the Tipple twins weren't looking forward to hearing it. If Aunt Maud ever had anything to moan about, it was the fact that her daughter had used her magic in public.

'We have a slight... p—' Aunt Maud began. Her teacup shook in her hand.

'Are you okay?' Mrs Tipple said.

'We have a slight problem. You see... Beatrice—'

'Oh, spit it out, Maud!' Uncle Patrick interrupted.

'Beatrice has used her magic again – this time at school.'

'That's awful!' Mrs Tipple said.

'That's not all,' Aunt Maud continued. Beatrice was leaning against the wall playing with her red hair. She looked pleased that she was the topic of conversation. On the other side of the room, however, strands of Aunt Maud's hair started sticking out at the sides. Mrs Tipple had told the twins before that this happened as a result of stress. It was something that happened to adults on a regular basis, only Aunt Maud was one of those unfortunate people it affected in a strange way.

'The other thing is… the head teacher saw it this time.'

'Oh, Maud,' Mrs Tipple said.

Mr Tipple and Uncle Patrick sat in a manly silence.

'What did the head say?' Mrs Tipple asked.

'He told us he saw Beatrice sending a year two pupil flying around the playground like a helicopter, and so did the rest of the school. But seeing this bizarre act… well, it sent him–'

'Oh spit it out, Maud!' Uncle Patrick whined.

Everyone sat straight and twiddled their thumbs, until a plate with some cookies on cracked due to Aunt Maud's tension and one of the sofas split in two. Uncle Patrick landed in a heap squirming and squealing like a pig.

'It sent him to a nuthouse!' she shouted. 'Patrick, get up off the floor. Stop being dramatic!'

'My suit, Maud! You've ruined my tailored suit! You know how long it took for them to get it to fit around my lumps and bumps!' he yelled, before squeezing himself comfortably in the crack of the now split-in-two sofa.

'Look, what I'm going to say to you is that my Beatrice is going to have to stay with you for a while,' Aunt Maud said as she took a hanky out of her posh handbag and dabbed the sweat from her forehead.

'No she's not!' Mr Tipple said, jumping up out of his chair, his mood smashing everyone's teacups.

'Well, that's rather rude!' Uncle Patrick also stood up, shaking the tea off his fingers. His bald head looked shiny under the light hanging from the ceiling, which eventually popped.

Aunt Maud started fake-crying loudly into her hanky. 'I'm sorry! I'm sorry, because you're not going to like what I have to say next,' she said, sobbing with one eye peering from behind the hanky. 'I've enrolled all three of them to start Chumsworth as of September, because I won't have my daughter go to Gospel Gluts.'

'Glums, Maud. It's Gospel Glums,' Mrs Tipple corrected her. 'Now come on, everyone calm down. We can't behave like this, not in front of the children. And control your magic moods!' she said, quickly turning the lamp on. 'Maud, it's fine, Beatrice can stay with us. She can't possibly go back home. It's far too dangerous. Though I can't say I'm happy with you interfering in my children's school life. No doubt you waved your money at the school to get them in? But you're right, Chumsworth is better than Gospel Glums.'

'Gluts, dear,' Maud said. 'It's Gospel Gluts…'

'Maud, where will you and Patrick go?' said Mrs Tipple, waving away Maud's last comment.

'Egypt!' shouted Uncle Patrick.

'Oh, but that's so far away?'

'Yes, we know it's… *further* away than normal,' Aunt Maud said, stabbing her umbrella into her husband's ribs. 'It's not like we ever got to see the sun really. Not since Beatrice was born. We should have known she'd be… difficult.'

She took the umbrella and handed it to Mrs Tipple like she was passing down the deed. She was already making moves to leave the Tipple house. Jenna and Jessica could tell this because she gave the house a look up and down with a disapproving scowl.

'So when will she move in?' Mrs Tipple said.

'Well, actually, we have her bags in the car. We really should get going. Our plane leaves in two hours. Patrick, get the bags will you?'

After Uncle Patrick came back soaking wet and holding onto the bags, which now had birds perched on them, Aunt Maud kissed Beatrice by rubbing noses, so as not to ruin her red lipstick. Mr Tipple took the bags off Uncle Patrick and Uncle Patrick disinfected his hands with a handy sized bottle of gel. Then they left.

'I hope she gets *really* wet,' Mr Tipple moaned. Beatrice was still leaning against the wall in the front room when the Tipples made their way back indoors. It was the end of a long day, and Mr and Mrs Tipple decided it was best she had their bed for now. They had to make do with the living room floor.

*

Jenna and Jessica lay in bed that night praying Beatrice would control her magic moods. They really didn't want to spend the rest of their childhood being cold and wet. But on the upside, there weren't as many birds on the square as there had been a few hours ago. Some of them had gone to Egypt with Aunt Maud and Uncle Patrick. But still… those magic moods.

CHAPTER FOUR

*

CHUMSWORTH

Jenna and Jessica were lying when they told Aunt Maud over the phone they enjoyed having Beatrice stay with them. Jessica nearly slipped up by asking Aunt Maud if she fancied taking Beatrice back. 'Ouch!' said Jessica, as Jenna gave her a sharp nudge in her side, which prompted Jessica to cover up. 'It's because she misses you… I think…'

Aunt Maud then told the girls that she and Uncle Patrick were at a fancy restaurant because they needed a break from lying on the beach all day. 'It's exhausting work, sunbathing,' Aunt Maud said. 'Honestly, I've never known exercise like it. You literally start sweating just by lying there.'

She also told the girls that the blackbirds that followed them had finally come into good use as they provided more shade around their hotel. The phone call didn't last long. Aunt Maud had to rush off because

Uncle Patrick had forgotten to order her a pudding on top of his five.

With their new guest staying, the Tipple twins had tried to get on as best they could with Beatrice. They nodded and smiled in the right places, which became quite depressing, to put it mildly. Not to mention the fact that one night they had caught Beatrice chasing Boo around her room, trying to use his loose ends as a blanket for her feet.

'You stupid white lump of nothing!' she cursed when she couldn't get her way. Boo hid in the wardrobe for a whole week afterwards.

Now it was the night before they started Chumsworth. The twins brushed their teeth looking at each other (instead of in the mirror) and tucked themselves up in their beds facing each other so they could fall asleep knowing what the other twin was doing.

Jessica had forgotten to take her odd socks off before jumping into bed, which usually would have bothered Jenna to breaking point, but the pair were so excited about the new emerald-green school uniforms that were laid out in front of them that nothing was going to bring them down. They had never worn a school uniform before. Gospel Glums made pupils wear their normal everyday clothes. Mr and Mrs Wilson had once stopped on their way to the car and stood stiffly, looking at the twins' colourful clothes they had chosen for school. Mr Wilson blocked Mrs Wilson's view with his chubby hands and said, 'What's this thing people call colour? Makes me feel strange.'

But the new school they were attending was different. The new school was strict. The new school didn't mess about when it came to order and principle. Chumsworth was the school every mother wanted their child to go to, and it had a headmistress called Miss Snippings, which was a very respectful name indeed.

'Don't go,' whispered Boo from under Jessica's bed.

'What do you mean, don't go?' asked Jenna.

'I don't like it. It's not safe. It's not safe,' said Boo, who seemed to be having a moment of panic.

'Boo, what are you talking about?'

Boo floated out from under Jessica's bed. 'It's dark, I tell you. Really dark.'

'What is?' demanded Jenna.

'Chumsworth… Chumsworth school!'

'Don't be silly, Boo. Chumsworth's the best sch—'

'No, no, it's not. Not for you two. It's black. I see black!'

'What do you mean, Boo?'

'Suffocating… I can't breathe… You can't breathe… Or someone else…'

'Boo, you're scaring me,' whimpered Jessica.

'Promise me you won't go?'

'We can't, Boo. We have to go. You know we do,' said Jenna.

'Then I'll be waiting every day for you to come home.'

'Yes, Boo. And we'll come and find you every day.'

This seemed to relax Boo a little, but it didn't stop him whispering a few words. 'Black, black walls, tightening… can't breathe…'

As the twins closed their eyes, little did they know that the blackbird perched on the chest of drawers had been there since the first morning it had arrived. It watched them silently and was still there the next morning when they awoke. They caught a glimpse of it from the corner of their eyes but thought nothing of it.

*

The September sun shone in the twins' eyes as they sat up the next morning. Nearly falling out of bed with excitement, Jenna and Jessica Tipple got up and continued their daily ritual of getting dressed together. It had been a long time since they had woken up feeling anything other than guilt about the fact their sister got taken and not them, and as a result it made all the furniture and other objects in their room dance and float in the air, lights switch on and off, and curtains open and close repeatedly.

'Must you go? I mean, really go?' asked Boo.

'Oh not this again,' said Jenna, sighing.

'But the darkness… it's the darkness. Shadows over walls…'

'Boo!' shouted Jenna. 'This has to stop. Until you can tell us exactly what it is.'

'But I can't. I don't know myself.'

'Well why don't we take you with us?' said Jessica. 'Will that make you feel better?'

'As if!' said Jenna. 'If we take Boo in, not only will we get into trouble, but nobody, and I mean *nobody*, is going to want to be our friend. Not when they see us rocking up with a dead person.'

'Nobody is going to want to be our friend anyway, Jenna, whether we turn up with a ghost or not. Everybody thinks we're weird.' She then turned to Boo. 'Remember, Boo, we'll find you when we get home,' said Jessica softly. They then left Boo and they went downstairs.

Without Aunt Maud's magic zap to help with Beatrice's weight over the last couple of months, Beatrice sat at the breakfast table looking quite deformed, with a half-skinny, half-fat body.

'Fancy a banana, Beatrice?' Mrs Tipple hinted, as she jerked her head around the kitchen door, looking red-faced and rather sweaty and holding a large parcel. 'Guess where this has just come from?' she snapped as she slammed down the heavy parcel and wiped the sweat off her nose. '*This* has just fallen from the sky in front of our house. Do you know how lucky we are that the neighbours didn't see! I mean, it's just ridiculous! Last week a parcel landed in the chimney, and the other day one actually walked to the door itself and knocked! Beatrice, you really need to stop telling your parents we're depriving you of luxuries in this house! Not only are they using their…' she lowered her voice, 'their *you know what* to deliver them, but we don't know where they're getting them from!' She then paused awkwardly when she saw that Beatrice had planted herself in Caitlyn's old chair.

Mrs Tipple tried to encourage Beatrice to shuffle along, and when this didn't work she resorted to speaking to her like a baby. 'You know, Beatrice, you're more than welcome to sit on the sofa in front of the tele and eat your brekky…or in your room maybe? Or how about outside with the birdies?' She gave up quickly when she saw that the blackbird in Jenna and Jessica's bedroom had in fact followed them down the stairs and was trying to sit on her shoulder. 'Oh for goodness' sake, what's the reason behind this?'

After breakfast, Beatrice opened her package, which contained a PlayStation and some games. By the time Mrs Tipple was ready to kiss them goodbye, Jenna, Jessica and Cousin Beatrice had already stumbled out of the front door, getting stuck, as arms and legs waved in every direction in a desperate attempt to try to be the first one out.

The blackbird flew from Mrs Tipple's shoulder and tried pulling the twins back with its beak. 'Oh look, it's trying to help,' she said, pulling the bird away by its wings and pushing the girls out of the door.

But the bird wasn't trying to help. In fact, it was trying to do the opposite. Jenna and Jessica realised that, as much as their mum hadn't. But they couldn't work out why. In all their years they had never known the birds to act in such a way. Yes, they confused the neighbours; yes, they repulsed the postman to the point where Bacton Square had a different postman almost every week. But had they ever tried to stop the girls from leaving Bacton Square? Never.

Finally, making their way through the birds outside, they each put up their umbrellas.

'That's not fair. I have one umbrella and they have two.'

'But Beatrice, they have one each, and two between them!' Mrs Tipple shouted from inside.

Beatrice stormed off ahead, her trousers now splitting as they made way for her growing body.

As the twins passed Mr Wilson's house, he was outside talking to Mrs Griffins about his breakfast. 'I had cornflakes this morning... soggy ones.'

Mrs Griffins had then snapped at the girls to run along and to never darken her doorstep again. 'Shoo! shoo!' she said, waving her hands as if they were birds themselves.

Moving along quickly, the twins left the square with one, two, three, and many more blackbirds leaving the rooftop to fly above them. This wasn't normal behaviour, but the twins ignored it all the same.

For people that didn't know the twins, it would seem that they didn't notice the 'MISSING' posters of Caitlyn posted on the red phone boxes and lamp posts. But this was far from true. Just reading the name 'Caitlyn Tipple' stabbed them in places they never knew they had. They had no choice but to keep their heads down and ignore such things.

They pretended to not see the pointing and whispering that came from others as they walked in time with each other.

To the Tipples' surprise, the blackbirds flying over them suddenly swooped down, landing on the pavement in front of them. The Tipple twins tried dodging and stepping over the birds but found it difficult. This only seemed to aggravate the birds more, as they were now squawking and flapping their wings harder.

Moving along through a huddle of birds, and occasionally bumping into strangers, the birds started pecking and pulling at their blazers and umbrellas.

'Oh these bloomin birds!' Jenna shouted, as Jessica tried frantically to pull them off them both.

A baby in a stroller pulled out its dummy and pointed at them. 'Mamma... tramps!' it said before it and its mum hurried off. Jessica felt this was aimed at her, mainly due to the fact she hadn't brushed her hair properly that morning. It was hard for some people.

Both uniforms were now ripped, their shoe laces tangled up and birds pulled at their shirts, nearly strangling them, causing Jenna and Jessica to bump into a lamp post and land in a muddy puddle, with one of Caitlyn's missing posters landing on top of them.

'That won't get her back, you know, ripping the posters down,' said a snotty passer-by.

Jenna and Jessica couldn't possibly turn up to Chumsworth looking like this on their first day, so they both went into the nearest shop, birds and all, and desperately tried to sort out their now ragged appearances. They had at least managed to shoo the birds away and ditch their umbrellas in a corner before the owner prodded them violently with his walking stick and they got thrown out. He chased them halfway down the street before they reached their destination: Chumsworth.

Chumsworth School was a grand building situated behind tall iron gates and railings in thick fog. The word 'CHUMSWORTH' was boldly displayed on top of those iron gates, which the twins found intimidating, to say the least.

They stood in front of the gates for at least a minute or two with their eyes and mouths open wide. There were blackbirds on the roof of the school. They told themselves it was just blackbirds that had followed them from their home, but no, they couldn't be, for these blackbirds had a more ghostly appearance than the ones at the Tipple house. They'd never seen blackbirds as ghostly as these before. But still, there was a possibility they could be birds from their house. That was the story Jenna and Jessica were sticking to. Then the gates opened on their own…

Swiftly moving through the gates and accepting it was perhaps their magic moods causing them to move, they made their way into the building, and it felt very odd to the twins, because, yes, it was raining and damp outside, but it wasn't freezing. And the minute they walked into the building it was so cold their legs were shaking and they found themselves blowing warm air into their hands to warm up.

They stood in the reception area of the school. A great school that achieved great things. And didn't this school know how to show it.

There was thick emerald-green carpet in all the corridors. The walls were decorated with some of the top work from the pupils, sports trophies, spelling contest trophies, school of the year trophies, and even a 'school to have the most trophies' trophy stood smack bang in the middle of them all, gleaming against the rest.

It wasn't long before they were disturbed by the school secretary, who they learned was called Mrs Greenose. She was a very orderly woman who had a rather large nose. She enjoyed her long nose, as it meant she could look down it at all the pupils.

'I take it you're the new girls,' she said, wiping a smudge off her glasses, but before Jenna and Jessica could answer, she continued. 'And I take it you've been told about room thirteen?'

'No, Miss,' said Jenna stiffly. Jenna and Jessica were suspicious of Mrs Greenose. In fact, they were suspicious of any stranger. Strangers had disappointed them. PC Dilks, for example, when he first entered the Tipple house, said he had high hopes of finding Caitlyn, as she wasn't a twin. Yet, years later, he had let them down. The whole world had let them down.

'Not one person has told you about room thirteen?' said Mrs Greenose impatiently, before waiting for an answer the twins didn't give. 'Oh dear. It appears there's a lot to catch up on then. I shall start by telling you very quickly that room thirteen... well, what can I say... You must not enter it, talk about it or have anything to do with it. No matter what goes on in this school, you must stay away from room thirteen.'

'But where is room thirteen?' the twins asked together.

'Uh! You just spoke about it. But to answer your question, I don't know where it is. That's one answer I haven't got,' Mrs Greenose said, ruffling through some papers. 'Nor has anybody, for that matter. Nobody knows *where* it is...'

'But—'

'No buts about it, girls… and you are *still* speaking about it. Give me one good reason why I shouldn't punish you right here, right now.'

Standing speechless, the twins decided they wanted to get away from Mrs Greenose as quickly as possible, so they changed the subject and asked where their class was.

Mrs Greenose checked her papers yet again and paused for a moment. 'Oh, how funny,' she said, sifting through them one by one. 'It says here you're both in the same class, but that can't be. You can't be the in the same class unless you're the same age. And to be the same age you have to be twins…'

'But, Miss, we are twins,' Jenna said, correcting her.

Mrs Greenose looked up slowly from her papers and studied the girls. 'My word! You are, aren't you. But not identical…'

'Yes, Miss, identical.'

'Identical twins at Chumsworth? But it can't be…' said Mrs Greenose, ruffling through her papers even more than before, until she gave up. 'I'll have to take your word for it, although Miss Snippings will despise this immensely. No twins have been allowed in here since the disappearances started. Miss Snippings won't have anything to do with them… it can hinder Chumsworth's reputation a great deal,' said Mrs Greenose, walking them up one of the long corridors to their class. They came to a halt when they finally reached it. 'Your teacher is called Mr Smith. He doesn't like lateness,' she said as she finally opened the door to let them in. 'So sorry, Mr Smith, I have the

new girls, Jenna and Jessica Tipple. They are twins, sir...
identical twins.'

'Yes, I know of the Tipple twins, thank you,' said Mr
Smith before Mrs Greenose left the room. 'Girls, if you
could come and stand at the front with me,' said Mr Smith,
showing them the way. Mr Smith was a slender man with
short, thick, wavy grey hair. He didn't care about the girls
being twins, nor did he care they were a Tipple. Jenna and
Jessica wished that everyone was more like Mr Smith.

'Now, before we start, I'd like everybody to get to
know Jenna and Jessica Tipple. Now, girls, are you okay
to talk about yourselves... maybe for the class to ask you
some questions?'

'Yes, okay,' said Jenna, pretending to be calm and
casual.

'And Jessica, what about you? Are you okay with this?'

'Well, all right then,' said Jessica without much
thought.

'I'll start!' said a small boy at the back of the class.

'Now, Tommy Grinch, you need to stick your hand
up first.'

'But I am, sir... See, I've got *both* hands up,' said
Tommy, reaching his hands up as high as he could force
them.

'Well, Master Grinch, fire away then.'

'You're those Tipple twins everybody talks about,
ain't ya? Are ya? Well?' Tommy said, leaning forward
impatiently. 'Is it true you're the only ones left? Are you
scared of the black figure? Do you think you're next? I
would if that were me.'

The twins shrugged awkwardly and looked at Mr Smith for reassurance.

'Now, Tommy, try and not talk about personal things, please.'

'But it's *hard*, sir. That's the stuff we want to know.'

'Okay, let's look at it like this. We all know about the black figure, but we want to know about Jenna and Jessica. The question *you* want to ask is… who are Jenna and Jessica?'

'The black figure, sir!'

'Okay, Tommy, considering you're adamant about this subject, maybe it would do the class some good if we had a group discussion about the black figure, but not singling our newcomers out. We all know this black figure exists and we don't really understand it, which is probably what scares us the most about it, which is okay because we as human beings find that if we don't understand something we get scared, and it's not just children that it happens to. Even we adults get scared of things that make no sense to us. Now, hands up… who is scared of the black figure?'

Jenna and Jessica looked around the room and saw that everybody had put up their hands. Everybody except for Tommy Grinch.

'I think I've seen the black figure before,' said Tommy, casually brushing his hair away from his eyes.

'Sir, Tommy's lying. He's not even a twin. Everybody knows the black figure only takes twins,' said a girl named Ruby, who was sitting at the front of the class.

'Now, Ruby, don't be so quick to judge. If Tommy has something to say, we need to listen.'

'The black figure doesn't just take twins. Caitlyn Tipple wasn't a twin, was she,' said Tommy angrily.

'Sir, Tommy's being personal, and you said we aren't allowed to say personal things,' stated Ruby quickly.

'Tommy, if we can just stick to your own experience, please,' said Mr Smith, who was now leaning against his desk.

'I swear I'm not lying! I saw it staring at me one night when I was eating my dinner. It was outside, it was. What have you got to say about that then, Ruby?'

'Carry on, Tommy,' said Mr Smith.

'I was like, "Oi, you there watching me eating. Yeah, you!" It didn't answer, so I stared at it with beady eyes. My mum asked me what I was doing and I told her I was seeing to a problem she needn't worry about.'

'So what happened next then, *Tommy*?' asked Ruby nastily.

'Well, I'll tell you what happened next. The black figure was no black figure any more. It had disappeared. And I finished my chips and treated myself to some more ketchup. I'm the man of the house and I'm not letting something that doesn't even seem to have a face or a real name put me off my food, thank you very much. Especially *chips*. Especially fish 'n' chip shop *chips*.'

'Well, thank you, Tommy, for your experience. I'm sure it's nice to know Jenna and Jessica aren't on their own when it comes to the black figure.'

'Thank you, sir,' said Tommy proudly.

Jenna and Jessica eventually got to sit down with the rest of the class and began to settle in, until they noticed something quite peculiar. It wasn't something they saw but something they smelt. If they'd had to describe it, they would have said it was a damp and musky sort of smell. A kind of smell that went straight up your nose and never came out again. A kind of smell that made Jenna finger flick.

They tried to snort the smell out and asked Tommy about it when he had them engrossed in ghost stories about Chumsworth as they sat in the corner on the carpet at the end of the school day.

'That's what that smell is,' said Tommy. 'It's ghosts.' Tommy was in his element, his green eyes wide. He told the twins stories about Miss Snippings. He said no one ever sees her and she is merely just a name above a door. And come to think of it, the twins had gone through the whole day and not seen her. They had no idea what she looked like or even what she sounded like for that matter.

Tommy raised his hands and scratched his face, which made the twins jump, and he told them Miss Snippings only came out at night to scratch on the doors of the children that had misbehaved that week in her school. Jessica said he was lying about that part, so he said he'd prove it one day by showing them the three scratches on a separate door inside room one – the caretaker's room.

'Jessica, I'll cross my heart and hope to die. I'm telling you, those scratches are indications of Miss Snippings' actions. She got hold of a child in room one and those scratches were all that was left of him. I wonder what's behind that second door.'

Tommy told them that if you did see her you had to turn around and touch the ground three times to get rid of a curse she might put upon you. He then scrunched his face and said, 'I reckon she's well ugly. I bet her toenails are as dirty as the day is long.'

But it was Jenna's and Jessica's faces that were scrunched when he mentioned, 'The hole of black'.

'The hole of black?' asked Jessica. 'What's the hole of black?'

'Oh, girls,' said Tommy in a condescending tone. 'The hole of black is Chumsworth's most feared punishment. No one, and I mean NO ONE, wants to get sent to the hole of black.'

'But what is it exactly?' enquired Jenna, who now felt so terrified she was unsure if she even wanted to know.

'It's exactly what it sounds like. A black hole in the ground. If you are naughty enough you get chucked down there... for hours... maybe even days.'

'Stop,' the twins said together.

'Some people come out of there not speaking. Some are too disturbed to even remember how to talk.'

'Stop!' they said again.

Tommy laughed. 'Okay, I'll stop. But just be warned.'

It was now quarter past three in the afternoon, and when Mr Smith had got the class silent, he asked the twins if they'd had a good first day and if they had any questions.

Jenna stood up first and asked if Miss Snippings was going to scratch on her door for being late that morning. Tommy put his head in his hands. 'Ah mate,' he mumbled to nobody.

Jessica then asked why there were blackbirds on Chumsworth's roof.

Mr Smith aimed his answer to the whole class and said, 'For the fiftieth time, Miss Snippings does *not* scratch on people's doors, and Jessica... there are no blackbirds on the roof.'

That night, Jenna and Jessica lay on their bedroom floor doing homework, but Jessica got distracted by the horrid thought of twins not normally going to Chumsworth.

'Maybe if we find Miss Snippings before she finds us... you know... to explain ourselves...'

'Jessica! We're not explaining to anybody about us being twins.'

Jessica shrugged it off. She thought her own opinion was fair enough. Then she realised she was falling behind with her work and decided to copy what Jenna had written for the rest of it.

CHAPTER FIVE

*

MEET MISS SNIPPINGS

Despite London being so miserable and bleak since Beatrice had moved to Bacton Square, there was a peculiar spell of sunshine over the weekend due to her mood lifting.

Of course, she'd had more parcels delivered to Bacton Square, so many that Mr and Mrs Tipple had trouble finding places to put the boxes before the binmen came. They shoved most of them up the chimney and under the stairs. The rest went on the roof and down the toilet.

Reports also came flooding in on the radio due to the abnormality of the hot weather. One was about a local girl who managed to catch some sun despite the odds being against her as she was classed as a typical pale Brit.

'Local Suzy Diphole is to be hailed as *Britain's Got Talent* winner even though she took no part in the show.

'Suzy Diphole, who is aged thirty-four, has been announced as next year's winner on the popular talent show for catching the most amount of sun in a rare seven-minute episode of clear skies. Suzy's husband has said that, "Nobody manages to catch that amount of sun, even when sunning it in Benidorm…"

'Suzy herself is also very pleased, as she has referred to herself as just a regular girl from London and never imagined she would achieve something as great as this. She said, "Just being a Brit and managing to get as tanned as I have during those seven minutes is a miracle – you know – because Brits normally only get burnt."

'It has been said that Suzy will stand before the queen on stage and reveal her tan for all of seven minutes to celebrate the seven minutes of sun time when she received the tan. She then said, "I think my next move after the show will be to travel to Spain or Cyprus to see how brown I really go. I'll put videos up on YouTube to show my skin's progress. That will be really interesting. I think…"'

The radio host then announced that if anyone was lucky enough to get burnt from the sun today, to call in and enter a lucky draw as the winner would receive ten thousand pounds.

It was Monday and Boo had waited patiently every day for the twins to arrive home, and he was most pleased when they arrived intact both physically and mentally. However, this didn't seem to stop him reeling off random words and acting worried. It wasn't that Jenna and Jessica didn't believe him. They just didn't think there was a lot they could do about it. They had to go to school.

Late again, they walked through the gates of Chumsworth and found themselves witnessing some very odd activity. It was moments after the gates closed behind them that this odd activity took place, and it consisted of what can only be described as the presence of another person coming from behind them. They couldn't feel it; they couldn't touch it. They definitely couldn't smell it, but yes, it was definitely there. However, when they turned to see who or what it was, they found nothing but the gates behind them. No person… just gates.

It wasn't until a little later that morning, at nine fifteen, that they thought they sensed something yet again – another person sitting between them on the carpet. So much so that when Mr Smith asked the twins who they wanted to work with, they both pointed to the unknown presence – at which point, Mr Smith assumed they were pointing at each other and paired them up together.

Feeling very peculiar about what had just happened and wondering why something had made them lift their hands and *point* so willingly to something they knew nothing about (if this thing ever actually existed), they moved to their desks with a suspicion that the extra person had now gone and started their work.

At lunchtime their stomachs were growling with hunger and they spent most of the walk to the canteen gossiping with Tommy about room thirteen. The three of them nearly didn't notice the drama happening all around them as they sat eating crisps and sandwiches. It was only when a pupil called Thomas Leary from year five mentioned their names that their ears pricked and their noses twitched.

'Well I wouldn't want to be those Tipple twins if you ask me.'

'Yes, I agree,' said another boy.

'What do you think is going to happen… you know… when we get there?'

The conversation quickly came to a halt when the group gossiping noticed prying eyes and ears.

'Come on,' said Tommy, standing up, 'we've got better things to do, haven't we…'

'Err… yes,' muttered Jenna, who was keen to get away quickly. 'Come on, Jessica,' she said to her sister, waving at her to stand up with them, before all three left the canteen together.

'If someone has something to say, they should just say it, eh?' said Tommy, as the three of them turned a corner and bumped into more gossiping groups of children swarming outside the hall.

Feeling eager to find out what it was that everybody was buzzing about, the twins and Tommy inched further through the crowds. Tommy, using his small height to an advantage, crawled to a group of older years and sat by their feet listening to what was being said.

'I can't believe it,' said a boy.

'Do you think it's *really* going to happen? I mean *really*?' said another.

'I don't know, but I'm glad I'm not Jenny McQueen. She said Miss Snippings scratched on her door the other month because she threw a pen across the room, and it hit her teacher on the head by accident.'

'Same as Johnny Ashwood. He got scratches on his door when he was late for class because he got his foot stuck in the toilet.'

'I don't know what I'm more worried about… the fact he got scratches on his door or the fact he had his foot in the toilet in the first place.'

'Miss Snippings might not say anything at all to them. Just because she's taking the assembly, it doesn't mean she's going to be talking about her scratching on doors.'

It was at this point that Tommy scampered from the floor and bolted towards Jenna and Jessica.

'You guys are never gonna guess what!' Tommy said, beaming.

'What?' said Jessica.

'It's Miss Snippings! She's going to be taking the assembly!'

*

Scrambling over their seats in the assembly hall, the twins and Tommy fought to be the one to sit in the middle. Giving up, Jenna moved to the other end of the row, which gave Jessica and Tommy no choice but to let her sit in the middle.

'I've gotta be honest, I'm glad I'm not you two right now,' whispered Tommy bitterly. 'Whatcha gonna do if Miss Snippings kicks you out when she sees she has twins in her school?'

'Don't bother me,' snapped Jenna unconvincingly.

'SILENCE!' screeched a sharp voice coming from behind them, causing the hairs on Jenna's and Jessica's necks to stand up. As everyone turned nervously to see who it was, they each saw an extremely tall woman with long fingers and wiry ginger hair. The woman wore a green scarf and walked down the aisle carrying a rigid yet twisted posture. Her hips stuck out slightly forward and her back was heavily hunched.

No one in the assembly dared move one tiny bit. In fact, the only movement the twins made was to sink further down into their chairs the moment the woman had passed them and took to the stage.

That woman was Miss Snippings, the headmistress of Chumsworth.

Miss Snippings sat down on a chair and took centre stage, but this chair was no ordinary chair… it was a *throne*. A colourful throne of green and gold. A throne indicating power.

After taking a moment to scan the room, Miss Snippings licked her soggy-looking lips and began speaking. 'Children! Pupils of Chumsworth!' she barked, spitting as far as the second row. 'Welcome back for another year! As I'm sure you are all aware, today's assembly will be about the All School Production!'

There were claps in the audience at the mention of the All School Production. Jenna and Jessica caught on slowly and clapped a little before Miss Snippings broke it up by slowly raising a finger.

'The All School Production! The show that every parent looks forward to at the end of the year. The show that promises entertainment and education rolled into one.' The pupils and teachers clapped again.

'Quiet!' Miss Snippings bellowed impatiently. 'This year's production shall be… shall be…'

It appeared to Jenna and Jessica that Miss Snippings had forgotten what it was she wanted to say. It was almost as if something had distracted her. Tommy shot a bewildered look at Jenna and Jessica, which they returned quickly.

'The All School Production shall be a show based on the Salem witch trials,' said Miss Snippings, finally picking up her pace again. 'A real-life horror story where normal people were accused of witchcraft, and which resulted in numerous executions.'

Miss Snippings then paused to lick her lips. But she didn't lick her lips in a normal sort of way. She licked her lips as if she had tasted something horrid. Her peculiar behaviour didn't end there. Miss Snippings sat silently on her throne scanning the room intensely with her grey eyes and suddenly straightened her back as if she'd never had a problem with her posture at all.

Feeling the urge to run and hide, Jenna and Jessica sat up stiffly in their chairs before sinking a little further down than before. Miss Snippings raised a long finger in the air slowly for a second time and opened her soggy-looking lips. 'Someone in this room has undermined my intelligence!' she shrieked. 'Someone in this room thinks they are a cut above the rest!'

Everyone looked at one another, confused , and Miss Snippings stood up and walked to the edge of the stage.

'Who in this school has been a naughty child?' she said, before making her way down the steps of the stage and moving closer to the rows of children.

'Is it YOU?' Miss Snippings shouted to a year one boy with yellow curly hair. 'Or YOU?' she snapped to a girl who had her hands placed neatly on her lap. Miss Snippings edged closer to the twins and closer still before screaming, 'IT'S YOU!' and pointing at Jessica, who was now twiddling her sweaty thumbs. 'You with the rosy cheeks... stand up!'

Jessica rose from her chair almost immediately. 'And why have I not seen you before?' enquired Miss Snippings.

'I'm... new, Miss,' shrieked Jessica uncontrollably.

'*New*? I haven't heard of any *new* children joining Chumsworth.'

'Yes, Miss. Just me and my sister, and cousin, Miss,' Jessica rattled, wishing she was anywhere but here.

'Sister? And where is this *sister* of yours? I want to see her,' said Miss Snippings. Jenna slowly rose from her chair, also struggling to make any sort of eye contact.

'And what is this we have here?' said Miss Snippings with great interest. 'Why, you're... T-T-T-T—'

'Twins?' added Jenna quickly to get it over with.

'Yes, twins!' screeched Miss Snippings. She tightened her wet lips so much they were nothing more than a wrinkled dot on her face. 'How dare these *things* enrol at my school without my permission!' barked Miss Snippings, and she hunched over again as if there was something about the word '*twins*' that she couldn't take any more.

Jenna and Jessica thought her bony figure looked like a tree in winter: all stick and no leaves.

'How dare these *things* enrol at Chumsworth! So... you thought you could enrol at Chumsworth without me noticing, did you?'

'No, Miss.' Jenna said bitterly. A weak attempt to argue back. Jessica could have killed her for this. Jessica knew Jenna didn't really know what she was doing. Miss Snippings scrunched up a little more.

'Let's see how clever you really are, shall we?'

'But, Miss—' said Jenna and Jessica together.

'Let me tell you this. Go unnoticed for the rest of the year and you can stay. If I hear just a peep out of either of you, I will make it extremely hard for you to come back next year. Have I made myself clear?' But before Jenna and Jessica answered, Miss Snippings snapped her hands together. 'Children! Back to your classes immediately! Assembly is over!'

As the children fled from the hall, Tommy found it hard to catch up with Jenna and Jessica, who managed to rush outside into the corridors before he did. 'Hey wait up!' he shouted before reaching them. 'Don't worry. It's not just you that people were looking at in there. That boy with the blonde hair who she picked on first... rumour has it he wet himself.'

CHAPTER SIX

*

THE HOLE OF BLACK

It was no reassurance to the twins that the blonde boy had maybe wet himself. In a way they thought he got off lightly. Chumsworth would forget that incident within a month... the twins however...

And why did Jenna think it was okay to answer back to the head? Jessica knew that Jenna was just as scared as she was. It was either an act of bravery or stupidity. Jessica couldn't decide. Either way, because of this, they had spent the last few weeks snapping at each other. Jenna knew Jessica was angry at her. But she was too stubborn to acknowledge it. Jessica decided to let it go. They had bigger issues to think about. One of them consisted of keeping their heads down and their eyes wide open. What with Miss Snippings' threats, they knew they weren't safe. They felt exposed to a predator. Victims. Was this what Caitlyn felt like on that night?

It was now the start of yet another week on a Monday. They had every intention of having a normal school day, but they ended up witnessing something quite bizarre. They had actually turned up to school on time as they had done every day since Miss Snippings had made her threats. They'd even gone through most of the day without feeling the strange presence that lingered about them.

Mr Smith had seated his class and told them to get out their books about the mysteries of the Salem witches (which the twins did willingly). The only thing that got on Jenna's nerves was the fact that Jessica's laces were not done up properly on her shoes. Jenna stared and stared, which made Jessica bend down to do them up. Jenna really needed Jessica to buck her ideas up sometimes. Jessica had always been a little scatty, but Jenna had noticed it worsen since the Caitlyn incident. Jenna sympathised with Jessica, she really did, but if Jenna didn't let Jessica know her laces weren't done up properly... who knew what would happen? Jessica might trip and fall. Jessica could end up dead.

'Now, before you open your book to the third page, I'm going to explain about the witches of Salem,' said Mr Smith, breaking Jenna's train of thought. 'As you've been told already, the witch trials were in fact a group of hearings and prosecutions of people who were accused of witchcraft in 1692. The Salem witch trials were terrifying times to live through. And we must all be thankful we don't live in them now.' Mr Smith then paused to clear his throat before carrying on. 'I'm going to start by telling you that the Salem witch trials were started by nothing more than a group of girls claiming to have been possessed by the devil, and they accused several women who lived locally of witchcraft. If you open your books to page three, you'll see something that the accusers were saying had happened to them.'

Jenna and Jessica opened their books and read…

Children who were inflicted by witches, sometimes made animal noises. For example, one child was found oinking like a pig. They could also burn up temperatures so high they would be sweating as if they've been cooked on a fire. One child was even found stiff, as if he had been stuck to his bed with super glue.

'Now, I'm going to begin by telling you about the four Goodwin children. Although these weren't part of the Salem witch trials, it actually happened in Boston before the Salem ones even began. But it's a good example of witchcraft, for they were said to have been inflicted by a witch. It's said that the witch had cast numerous spells on them.'

'Like what, sir?' asked a boy in the middle row.

'Well, some people say they were found purring like cats and barking like dogs.'

'That's insane, sir,' said the boy.

'That's not all. Some say that the witches had bent and snapped their bones into funny shapes. So much so they no longer looked like human beings but more like broken puppets.'

'That's horrid!' the children cried.

'I haven't finished. They were so tormented they were found flying in the air like birds. They soared and swooped and looped the loop! They soared so high they could see the whole of Salem underneath them.'

'What else, sir? Tell us more! Tell us more!' cried the children.

'All right then, but just one more,' said Mr Smith, taking a seat at his desk. 'There's the story of Betty Parris. Betty Parris was a girl who suddenly became ill. She said she felt as if she had caught the flu but seemed perfectly fine when she decided to dive under furniture and dash about like a headless chicken.'

The class laughed.

'She dived under the beds. She dived under the kitchen table. She dived so much it was as if she was a dolphin in the sea.'

'That's funny, sir,' said Ruby.

'In fact, while we're talking about it, I'd like to inform you it was she and her cousin Abigail Williams that started these stories and lies. They would act as if they were being tortured by a witch and blamed certain women who lived locally of doing it. These women were called Tituba, Sarah Good, Sarah Osborne and Martha Carrier. Martha was later found guilty of being a witch and was sentenced to death.'

'That's awful,' said Ruby.

'Now, we all know that these stories are made up and I don't think we will ever truly know the reason that started it all. I can assure you now that if this happened today, nobody would believe it'

'I might,' said Tommy from the back.

'No you wouldn't,' muttered Ruby from the front.

'Now, now class, this wasn't just something that happened at playtime. These were stories that got so out of control that these people stood up in front of a judge in court and claimed such lies. If you go to the next page, you will see a script from the court hearing.'

JUDGE: Abigail Williams, who is causing you pain?
ABIGAIL WILLIAMS: Martha Carrier. She says she will pull my hair and burn my skin if I do not do what she tells me.

Mr Smith opened his mouth to speak but their lesson was interrupted when the children heard a deathly scream coming from outside in the corridor. Shocked, Mr Smith and the class ran out to see what was going on only to see a year six girl lying on the floor face down. She was grunting words that didn't make sense and her body was convulsing. Jenna and Jessica walked over to her to try and help her up, and the minute Jenna's hand touched the girl, she stopped fitting.

Mr Smith then tried turning the girl over, and when he was successful the girl came to her senses. She screamed, 'It was them! It was those two!' and pointed accusingly at the twins.

'What was them? They've been in my class the whole time.'

'It was! It was! It was!' the girl screamed. 'They blocked my way,' she said, sobbing. 'They made me fall.'

'Oh yeah? And how did they make you fall if they weren't here, eh?' Tommy said when he shoved his way to the front of the crowd. 'You can't say they pushed you.'

'No, no, they just stood there staring till I fell. They blocked my way and wouldn't let me past. They spoke to me using their minds and not their mouths, and they told me to do things I didn't want to do.'

'This is an outrageous accusation!' Mr Smith cried, and then he paused. 'But come to think of it, where were you? You've been quiet all day.'

The twins pleaded with Mr Smith to try to get him to remember that he was in fact teaching them stories, with events just like this one, but for the life of him he couldn't remember.

It was when Miss Snippings appeared from nowhere that the twins knew this was going somewhere they wouldn't like.

'Bring them to me!' she screeched from the far end of the corridor, her orange hair glowing in the shadows. The crowd of children parted, making a large aisle for the Tipple twins to walk down, which they did shakily.

Miss Snippings looked at the twins and a cruel grin broke out on her face. 'So you think you can pull a stunt like that without getting caught?'

The twins backed away, cowering from her.

'There is only one punishment for girls like you, and that is THE HOLE OF BLACK!' Miss Snippings cried.

There were gasps of shock from the other children. Jenna had decided to make a run for it but thought better of it when Miss Snippings seized them both by the scruffs of their necks and dragged them outside and to the rear of the playing fields.

'Surely this is uncalled for,' Mr Smith said to Miss Snippings, as he tried desperately to keep up.

Miss Snippings seemed not to hear anything anyone was saying. In fact, she seemed as if she was having quite a good day. And when it came to throwing the twins down the hole, she told them to mind their heads and laughed uncontrollably when she slammed the bars down.

Jenna and Jessica sat in what was nothing but a soggy hole in the ground filled with mud. They were wet, cold and scared. This was without a doubt the most degrading moment of their life. Staying in a hole… for an hour… until school had ended.

*

It was now November and the smell of the cold, smoky air outside only reminded the twins that Christmas was just around the corner. A time which made the twins think about Caitlyn more often. And a time when they realised they would be spending another Christmas without her. If only they hadn't woken her that night. If only Caitlyn hadn't gone outside.

It was late afternoon, and Jenna and Jessica could hear their mum downstairs. She was bickering on the phone to Aunt Maud and she sounded as if she'd had enough. Not only did she raise her voice for Jenna and Jessica to hear but she raised it for the whole of Bacton Square to hear also.

Mr Wilson knocked on the door, his fist making the most mundane knock one could make. But when Mrs Tipple opened the door and stood there with a blackbird perched on her head, Boo cradled in one arm and the phone clamped between her shoulder and ear, he knew he had no chance of complaining about the noise. He stood silently for a while, quaking and shivering with fright at the sight of Boo and the bird, until he jumped the iron railings back to his home next door.

She slammed the door shut and the twins quickly crept to the top of the stairs to listen to what she was saying to Maud down the phone, when they noticed a nose and eyes sticking out of the wallpaper. It was Beatrice. She had turned herself into the same print as the wall so she could earwig on Mr and Mrs Tipple without being seen. 'I won't tell if you won't,' said Beatrice cautiously.

'You'll never guess what Maud has done now,' Jenna and Jessica heard their mum say to their dad from downstairs, finishing her phone call with Aunt Maud. 'She's only gone and moved to America without telling anyone. Apparently... she's got into a spot of bother there now and wants to visit for a few weeks... until the New Year. Oh, but it will be okay, according to *Maud*. She reckons we should have a present turn up any minute now to make up for the extra stress she has put on us.'

Jenna, Jessica and Beatrice were listening more intently, causing Beatrice to kick Jenna in the shins.

'Ouch!'

'I can feel you breathing on me – stop!'

There was another knock on the front door.

It looked like their gift from Aunt Maud was already waiting outside. The twins scampered off the landing and went back into their rooms. Beatrice remained standing against the wall. 'Pssst, you two! Pssst. I'm stuck!' Beatrice had stupidly plastered herself to the décor instead of just camouflaging herself with it.

By the time the twins went back out to help, it was too late, as their mum was already opening the front door again. She opened it aggressively, probably thinking it was Mr Wilson again, only she was very shocked to see that, instead, in walked a miniature Yorkshire terrier with a note stuck to its collar.

Jenna and Jessica excitedly rushed downstairs while their mum placed Boo in mid-air and grabbed the Yorkie before reading the note out loud.

'My name is Oliver. I'm your new furry friend. P.S. Please forgive Aunt Maud and Uncle Patrick.'

They took Oliver into the living room and made a fuss of him.

'Where's Beatrice?' asked Mrs Tipple. 'Beatrice, come downstairs, will you!' she shouted.

'Oh, the thing about Beatrice is... well, she's sort of stuck,' Jessica said before hinting they might need a wallpaper scraper to get her out.

'Is this true, Jenna?' asked Mrs Tipple.

'Yep,' replied Jenna, before they each made their way back to the top of the staircase.

Struggling with all his might, Mr Tipple soaked Beatrice until she was soggy to the bone and carefully tried peeling her off limb by limb. Beatrice was now crying and moaning she was claustrophobic. Jenna and Jessica could see their cousin was in a sweaty state, and in return she was causing them to be the same. As they tried to concentrate on the soaking wet wallpaper, images came flooding over them. Images of feeling stuck. Images of being locked in the dark.

The hole of black, to be precise.

After tantrums, cups of tea and an exchange of nasty names, Mr Tipple finally released Beatrice from the wall. 'The next time you pull a stunt like that you can stay there!' he snapped as he stomped down the hall and into the kitchen. He came to a halt when he saw the kitchen table covered with delicious food. Roast beef, crispy roast potatoes, all the veg you could want, home-made bread, jugs of gravy and glasses of wine. Oliver was sitting at the kitchen table holding a knife and fork in his paws, nodding towards the food for the family to enjoy, which he had just made.

The Tipples decided to take advantage of Oliver's peculiar ways for just one night. After that, Mrs Tipple insisted on training him to act like a dog and not like a person.

By the time Oliver had washed up and took himself for a walk, it was night-time already. The twins crept into their beds and pressed their cheeks against their pillows. Their attention turned to Miss Snippings and the mysterious ways of Chumsworth. What was the presence that followed them? What did it want from them? And why did Miss Snippings hate them so much? Also, why had the girl accused them of doing things they hadn't done?

After an hour of dwelling over the answers, they still weren't hopeful. They tossed and turned until eventually they fell asleep.

CHAPTER SEVEN

*

TO THE GALLOWS

When they awoke the next morning, Oliver was standing at the ends of their beds with breakfast already made. Eggs and bacon.

Jenna and Jessica had overslept. Their eyes were heavy and swollen, and their hair... had seen better days. When Jenna and Jessica looked in the mirror they thought they looked as if they were auditioning for a part in a zombie movie. Had this been the case they would have won the day already. But this wasn't the case. They were going to Chumsworth. They had to sort themselves out.

Gulping down their breakfast and putting on their uniforms, they were ready in no time and dashed out the door with neat-ish hair and their clothes looking scruffy.

They each blew a sigh of relief when they bumped into Tommy at the gates. They needed an extra body by their side. Some sort of protection. However, if Jenna and Jessica were honest with themselves, they knew that no number of people could protect them from Miss Snippings.

Tottering off into the building, they followed the crowd of pupils. But instead of parting to go to individual classes, the crowd stayed together and made for the hall.

'I forgot to say,' said Tommy quietly, 'Miss Snippings wants to take another assembly. Wonder what that's all about, eh?'

Jenna and Jessica didn't answer. What could they say? How stomach-wrenching would it be? How they wished they could go in the opposite direction and simply leg it. In all honesty they didn't know what to say. All they could do was hope for the best.

Moving along with the other pupils, they entered the hall and saw a petrifying image. Miss Snippings was already on the stage, perched upon her throne, but she was stonily silent as she waited for the pupils to fill the hall. There wasn't a sound, just silence.

Miss Snippings waited for a minute or two before she rose from her chair and looked around the hall. Focusing on the children, she took a breath and began to speak.

'Good Morning, children.'

'Good morning, Miss Snippings,' the children chanted back.

'I'm going to begin this assembly today with a question. And that question is this. What is a witch?' she asked slowly. 'A witch…' she stated again, before pacing the stage. 'When you hear that word, what springs to mind?'

Nothing but gormless expressions answered her question.

'Let me guess,' she said. 'Is it a woman with a green face? A black cat that sits by her side? Someone who brews wicked spells over a cauldron? Or is it someone who has warts on her face? There are so many stereotypes of a witch, but what I'm going to tell you today is something not from fairy tales but something very real. Today, I'm going to tell you the story of the witches of Salem.' She froze, waiting for some sort of reaction, yet there was none.

Jenna and Jessica thought she looked like she wanted attention. Like she thought she was the star of a show, but to the twins she was no star, more a total eclipse.

'A real witch is actually somebody that is no different from you and me. A witch is somebody that looks the same, acts the same and dresses the same. But it's what witches *do* that separates them from the rest. Witches have the ability to step away from their own bodies and travel in spirit form. They have the ability to cause disasters while standing at a distance. They also have the ability to poison a person just by one evil glance!

'I'm going to start this story at the very beginning. The story has captured attention for many years now, and still to this day it's not clear why it happened.

'January 12th in 1692 was the date of the first recorded incident. It was the first day of... what can we call it? Peculiar activity?' Miss Snippings made her fingers into a fist. 'Yes, that's it... peculiar activity. It was a cold snowy day and a few men were travelling from Salem village to Salem town. When they got to the town they found a woman who went by the name of Alice Parker. Alice Parker was lying outside her home as if she were dead. There was a lot of fuss from the public as they crowded around her. "Help!" they cried. "Help Alice Parker!" But the men were dubious to pick her up. It was odd to them that a woman was lying in the snow for no obvious reason.

'One of the neighbours then told the men that Alice Parker had been unconscious many times before, so there was no need to worry, and yet the men were still jittery about touching her, until one eventually gave in and lifted her over his shoulder to take her inside.

'Before he got to the door he dropped her once or twice on the snow by accident and yet she still remained asleep. Nothing woke her up. She didn't even mumble or open an eye. When he finally got her inside and put her to bed, she sat up suddenly. Her back was rigid and stiff. One man claimed to have heard a snapping sound as she tried to twist in different directions. But that wasn't all. You would think Alice Parker would thank the men for helping her, but she didn't, for she did nothing but laugh loudly at them. She cackled and cackled and cackled so much her head looked like it was going to pop. It was as if there had never been anything wrong with Alice.

'But suspicion has it that Alice was a witch and she had managed to separate her spirit from her body and cause trouble elsewhere while her actual body was lying in the snow.' Miss Snippings stopped for a moment. 'Anybody else find it strange that a woman who was possibly ill was seen as a witch? But then why would she laugh? Why didn't she thank the men? You can see how they might have come to that conclusion.

'Now, as I have said before, that was the very first recorded incident – this is why I've chosen to tell you about it. But the story I'm going to move onto next is the story of Tituba, because it only happened just three days afterwards in Salem village. It's a wonder that two women, one from Salem village, one from Salem town, experienced these odd things within just days of each other – and they didn't know one another either.'

Miss Snippings paced slowly with a finger on her lips, looking as if she was thinking of how to start, when her eyes lit up suddenly.

'Tituba, who was a slave, worked for Samuel Parris in the family home, where she looked after his nine-year-old daughter Betty Parris and his niece Abigail Williams, who was eleven. It was Friday 15th January 1692, and Tituba had spent the day going about her usual business and duties, when Tituba was said to have seen a whirl of black air and dust fall all around her, which put her into a deep sleep.

'During this sleep, Tituba had seen a tall dark man standing next to her. Although the man was so dark he could have almost been hidden in a shadow, there was one thing about him that stood out. He had a long white beard. This long white beard glowed in the darkness of the room and seemed to have had some sort of hypnotic hold over Tituba. She felt it was calling her to listen, to trust the man. The beard was enticing her. Then the man opened his mouth and told Tituba something unpleasant.

'He said that he wanted to kill the children in the home and demanded Tituba help him or he would kill her too. He told her he was a god, somebody she should believe in. He then produced a document from beneath his beard and put it in front of her. He told her that if she served him for six years, and six years only, he would give her all the riches in the world and she would be a slave no more.

'He illustrated this by lighting up the room as if it was awash with gold. Gems and diamonds covered the floor. But if she refused... he told her he would treat her in the way he planned to treat the children in the Parris's home, and eventually Tituba would live no more.

'Waking up and finding herself in the same room she had fallen asleep in, Tituba was unsure of what she had just seen. She decided to put it behind her, but the next day the man came again, though not in the form of a man, but as birds. Green birds, yellow birds and white birds. Tituba told the flock of birds, "No", but they carried on flapping around her. "Serve us... serve us now," said the birds, but Tituba refused. She said she wouldn't serve him and ran out of the room. She said she would go and tell her master, Samuel Parris, what was happening, but she was stopped aggressively (although not by the flock of birds, for they had transformed back into the man) and he told her to serve him *now*. He then said he would be back on Wednesday.

'It appeared that the man had already begun inflicting things on the children, for they had been acting strangely a little earlier that day. They would hide under furniture, and their postures would be twisted.

'When it was Wednesday (20th January), the man returned when Betty and Abigail were in a room with their parents and Tituba was in another room. The man appeared before Tituba, but he wasn't on his own. He had brought four floating women with him. The man grabbed Tituba roughly and told her to pinch the children.

'Tituba shook her head, for she couldn't hurt innocent children. This made the man angry and he told the four floating women to drag Tituba to the room where the little girls were.

'Being too scared to fight the four women off, Tituba let them take her into the room and across to the other side with the man following behind.

'It appeared to Tituba that the man had enchanted Betty, Abigail and Mr and Mrs Parris because none of them acted as if they had seen the six walk across the room. "I won't do it," said Tituba, but the four women forced her to stand before the girls and made her pinch them repeatedly. Betty and Abigail screamed with pain and asked for it to stop. However, it was some time before it did.

'Afterwards, the women left, but the man didn't, for he had unfinished business with Tituba. He promised to return on Friday and told her he would bring his book back for her to sign, and he made clear he only needed her for six years.

'But come Friday 22nd January, the man returned with his book but was unsuccessful in persuading Tituba to sign it. He had a pin with him that he told her to prick her finger with and sign his book in her blood, only he was interrupted when Mrs Parris called up to Tituba from downstairs and the man vanished. Relieved, Tituba went to bed that night but knew she wouldn't be free of the man. If only she could find a way to end his wicked ways.

'On the Saturday, Tituba was mopping the floor, when, to her displeasure, she felt she was being watched. There seemed to be something hiding in the shadows in the far corner of the room. Tituba watched closely until she could make out what it was, when a red cat jumped from the shadows and shouted "Serve me". The cat then changed into the shape of the man.

'The man carried a yellow bird with him and the four women were also by his side, only this time Tituba recognised two of them as people she had known. They went by the names of Sarah Good and Sarah Osborne of Salem village.

'The man presented Tituba with his book again and demanded her to sign it with her blood. When she looked through the pages of the book, she noticed there were nine other names signed in blood. Some of the blood was red, some yellowish. Two of the names she noticed were Sarah Good and Sarah Osborne. Tituba asked the two women she recognised why they had signed the book and they replied, "He is our master now, for he has promised us a life of luxury once we have served him."

'Tituba again refused, and the man threatened to do much damage to Betty and Abigail before leaving.

'By the time it was late February, it was clear that the man had kept his word, because Betty and Abigail hadn't improved, they had worsened. They cried of headaches, threw fits and sometimes their bodies seemed so weak it was as if they had no bones in them. It was on 25th February when Tituba had had enough of seeing Betty and Abigail in this state and decided to take it upon herself to kill the demon that was tormenting them. She made a cake using the girls' urine, for she believed that the demon lived inside the girls, and by taking the urine out of their bodies, it would mean taking out the demon. If Tituba could get an animal to eat the urine baked in the cake, it would mean the animal would be eating the demon.

'She gave the cake to a dog and the dog lapped it up nicely. But later that day the girls' condition had worsened. They blamed Tituba for their pain. Their necks and backs had twisted into unusual positions.

'By Monday 29th February, Tituba had been arrested for witchcraft. However!' Miss Snippings snapped, causing everyone in the hall to jump, 'Tituba was not sentenced to death. This is where it gets interesting!' she said, raising her voice. 'Tituba was innocent. Tituba did not sign herself over to the devil. And yet, do you know what she did?' Miss Snippings asked, before sniggering into her scarf. 'She confessed! That's it – *she* confessed.' Miss Snippings' sniggering turned into outrageous laughter. 'Poor little Tituba confessed to witchcraft and she was let off. Who confesses to a crime they didn't commit?' Miss Snippings was now holding her stomach tightly. Miss Snippings was laughing hysterically. Some of those in the hall started to laugh with her, uncomfortably, because they felt that if they didn't… they would be in trouble.

'And what do you think of that then?' she asked, her mood a little bitter now.

'I said, what *do you* think of *that?*' she snapped impatiently, leaving her voice to echo around the room. The pupils' laughter faded a little as Miss Snippings' tone became more serious.

'Right… okay… the next part I'm not going to tell you,' she said to the children, who were growing restless. 'I'm going to act it out. *We* are going to act it out. Yes, that's it. *We* are going to act it out!' said Miss Snippings fervently. Miss Snippings looked as if she had just come up with a cunning plan. 'I need two volunteers to come up and act it out!' she barked. 'I'm going to pick!' she said excitedly as all those in the hall trembled with fear. 'Who wants to be my guinea pig!' she shrieked. 'I know! The Tipple twins! Who would like to see the Tipple twins act out the next part of the story?' Miss Snippings cried even more excitedly. It was as if she was about to burst. 'Come up! Come up to the stage!'

Jenna and Jessica got up off their chairs and walked towards Miss Snippings. Jenna, who was struggling to control her anger as she got closer to the head, began biting her lip to prevent herself from making rude remarks. Jessica, on the other hand, stared at Miss Snippings. She lost focus when she caught a glimpse of a gap in Miss Snippings' teeth and wondered how many pennies she could fit in it.

'Quickly, quickly!' Miss Snippings cried. Jenna and Jessica stood by Miss Snippings, who was now looking as if she had cooked herself up a tasty treat. 'Do you know what happened to a witch after she was tried for witchcraft? Do you know what the punishment would normally be?' asked Miss Snippings. 'Tituba was lucky, she got off, but others accused of witchcraft were executed, sentenced to death! They were sent to Gallows Hill, where they each met their end.'

Jenna and Jessica just stared at the audience in front of them.

'I'm going to be the judge. You two are the witches.' Miss Snippings couldn't contain herself. She was already in the moment. 'I sentence you, Jenna and Jessica, to be hung! Now go to Gallows Hill!'

Jenna and Jessica looked up at Miss Snippings, puzzled.

'Go!' she cried. 'Stamp your feet! You have just been sentenced to death! Now go to Gallows Hill!'

Jenna and Jessica stamped up and down, pretending to walk to Gallows Hill.

'Now jump in the air! Cry out your innocence!'

'What?' asked Jenna angrily.

'Jump up and down, up and down!'

Jenna and Jessica jumped up and down.

'Now spin around! Spin around! The rope is tight!'

'But...'

'I said spin!'

Jenna and Jessica spun.

'Faster!'

They spun faster.

'You're not doing it properly! You're not choking!'

Jenna and Jessica gagged a bit.

'MORE! MORE!'

'We can't!'

'I SAID MORE!'

Jenna and Jessica gagged and spun, and before they knew it, they felt their toes being raised from the ground. Gasps came from the audience as they rose higher and higher.

'Look!' cried a child.

'They're flying!' cried another.

'They are witches!' said a few.

'No, Miss Snippings is! Miss Snippings is the witch!' someone screamed.

Jenna and Jessica dropped to the ground suddenly when Miss Snippings looked out at the audience.

'Who said that?' she asked everyone in the hall. 'Somebody called me a witch. Who was it?'

'It was me, Miss,' said a plump boy with ginger hair. Jenna and Jessica recognised him as someone from the year below them.

'Stand up!' shrieked Miss Snippings.

The ginger boy stood up.

'Are you telling me you are accusing me of being a witch?'

'No, Miss,' said the boy.

'Then why did you say it?'

'I don't know, Miss,' said the boy twiddling his hands around his sides.

'And what would you say if I told you this was set up?'

'I don't know what you mean, Miss.'

'I mean it has been staged. Jenna and Jessica weren't

flying in the air, they were held up by pieces of string. It's something we planned together before this assembly began. Isn't that right?' said Miss Snippings, as she shot a cold look at the twins.

Jenna and Jessica had to lie. They weren't held up by string – this hadn't been planned or rehearsed. But could they turn on Miss Snippings? Not if they valued their lives.

'Yes, that's right,' they said together.

Miss Snippings began sniggering in her scarf again. She began laughing at the twins and they knew why. It was the same reason she'd laughed at Tituba – for admitting to something they hadn't done, to free themselves from evil.

Miss Snippings laughed and cackled, and cackled some more, until everyone in the hall joined in and laughed along with her. Chumsworth students were pointing and laughing and laughing and pointing.

Jenna and Jessica could take it no more. Jessica ran off the stage and Jenna ran after her.

Reaching the toilets, Jessica flung herself into the nearest cubicle.

'We can't hide in here. I think Miss Snippings has released everyone from assembly. I can hear footsteps,' said Jenna, peering out of the cubicle door. 'This place is gonna be packed really soon.'

'I know,' said Jessica, blowing her nose before a group of girls came in and stared at Jessica's tearful face.

'Serves you right,' said the taller one. 'After what you've both been doing in people's homes.'

'What does that mean?' asked Jenna.

'You know what you've been doing. That's probably why Miss Snippings hung you out to dry on that stage,' said the girl, and she walked back out with her group behind her.

'Girls, come on,' said Tommy, barging in. 'Jessica, I know you're upset, but don't let Miss Snippings win. She can't keep doing this to you. First of all the hole of black, then this. It's not on. Don't let her know it bothers you.'

Jessica looked at Tommy. He was right.

'But what about those girls? One of them said something about us doing things in people's homes?'

'People's homes?'

'Yeah.'

'I ain't got a clue, but we gotta get out of here quick. I can't be seen in the girls' loos.'

Jenna, Jessica and Tommy darted out of the toilets and spent the rest of the day isolating themselves by sitting at the back during carpet time and huddling in corners during lunch. They didn't see Miss Snippings for the rest of the day. This wasn't any comfort to Jenna and Jessica. They knew it was only a just matter of time before they saw her again.

CHAPTER EIGHT

★

VANISHED

When Jenna and Jessica finished their day at Chumsworth they couldn't get home quick enough. They needed the safety of their bedroom and the warmth of their family and they needed it now.

'It happened, didn't it?' said Boo, trembling by the window as the twins entered their bedroom. 'You know… the suffocating.'

'Yes. Yes it did,' the twins said together. They thought that perhaps that's what Boo had meant when he had his little panic attack – that night in their room, when he wailed on about somebody suffocating. That moment Miss Snippings made them act out being hung.

'Are you going to go back?' said Boo wearily.

'Of course we are,' said Jenna.

'I don't think that's wise,' said Boo.

'We don't have a choice,' said Jessica as she slumped on her bed. She knew it was normal for children to despise school, but this was on another level. Not only were they paranoid about what Miss Snippings might do next, but they were now worried about what others were saying.

Was this really happening? Were they going mad? And yet there was no way out. Jenna and Jessica both felt they had to put up and shut up.

*

It was now the first of December. It was dark outside in the early hours of the morning, and Oliver had barked and barked until eventually Mrs Tipple got out of bed.

When she peered through a half-open eye, she saw that the time was four thirty in the morning. Oliver barked even more now knowing she was awake, and she plodded through the living room and slipped over a puddle of wee in the hallway before letting him outside. Oliver ran out into the foggy mist before she had a chance to shout at him. She then closed the door quickly before letting in any more crisp air from outside.

It was five o'clock in the morning when Oliver returned from his walk. He marched straight past her into the kitchen and drank her coffee that she'd made.

When she finally put Oliver's dog food in a bowl for him, he tossed it aside and began making his very own fry-up while listening to the radio.

Exhausted, she snatched the eggs and bacon from under Oliver's nose and reached across the table to switch the music off. 'Bad Oliver!' she yelled, and Oliver stormed out of the kitchen, slamming the door behind him.

He sulked upstairs for twenty minutes until he decided he wanted to return. He came down the stairs wearing a baseball cap and a bomber jacket and started making the most awful noise by the front door. He was building his very own cat flap.

At ten o'clock, the twins couldn't believe their luck when their mum and dad got the Christmas tree out of the loft. Mrs Tipple wanted to put it up before Aunt Maud and Uncle Patrick returned, in case they interfered.

Oliver ran around the living room wearing a Christmas hat, while the twins and Beatrice covered him in tinsel and chased after him.

When all the decorations were up, Mr Tipple moved the tree right in the corner by the window, its lights beaming into the shadows of the room.

By the time Aunt Maud and Uncle Patrick arrived, it was three thirty in the afternoon. Aunt Maud didn't knock this time. She stood outside, soaking wet and shivering with her face planted against the living room window. When Mrs Tipple finally went to the door to let them in, Aunt Maud barged past her, her orange skin outshining the Christmas lights, her face resembling an angry pumpkin.

'What have you done to my Beatrice?'

Mrs Tipple began to explain, only to be interrupted by Aunt Maud.

'She's nearly *double* the size of me and is the first thing you see through the window! I want my daughter to look like an angel, the star above the tree... NOT FATHER

CHRISTMAS!' Aunt Maud collapsed onto the sofa, squashing Oliver under her peachy bum and her wet bags. 'I don't know who she looks like more, Patrick, I really don't. It's either Santa Claus himself or his sack of presents.'

'Well, sack of presents, Maud. Does she look jolly? Can't you see her clothes hugging her figure like a bag of potatoes?'

Aunt Maud stuck her finger out in front of her and struck Beatrice with incredible force. Beatrice coughed at the smoke that lingered around her and saw she was her skinny self again. 'Thanks, Mum,' she said, as she headed off into the kitchen to fetch a bowl of chocolates. Oliver had escaped from beneath Aunt Maud's bottom and ran outside.

*

A little later, when they were halfway through eating the dinner in the living room, somebody knocked on the door.

'Oliver?' Mrs Tipple said, as she wondered who it could be.

Jenna stood up and pressed her nose against the cold window. 'No, Mum, he's hanging around with teenagers on bikes.'

Mrs Tipple then went and answered the door, and when she came back she looked all flustered. A policeman walked in behind her. Aunt Maud spat out her mashed potatoes and kicked Uncle Patrick in the ribs. (who was eating his dinner sat on the floor whilst playing on the

PlayStation). The Tipple twins recognised the policeman straight away. They had seen his dark hair, sharp nose and chubby body before. It was PC Dilks, the officer in charge of Caitlyn's disappearance.

'You might want to sit down,' he said, looking seriously at Mr and Mrs Tipple.

They sat down holding each other's hands. When they were as comfortable as they could be, Mrs Tipple plucked up the courage and asked weakly, 'What is it? What have you found?'

'This isn't about Caitlyn, I'm afraid.'

'No?' Mrs Tipple said.

'No?' Aunt Maud repeated, giving sharp looks to PC Dilks and Uncle Patrick.

Uncle Patrick kicked the PlayStation that was sprawled across the floor underneath the telly with his left foot and smiled at PC Dilks. 'So, you all ready for Christmas then?' he said.

Ignoring Uncle Patrick's question, PC Dilks continued talking to Mr and Mrs Tipple.

'I'm afraid we've had some complaints.'

'What about? I've done nothing wrong!' Uncle Patrick snapped.

'No, neither have I,' Aunt Maud butted in.

'It's about Jenna and Jessica,' PC Dilks said to no one in particular.

'What about them?' Mrs Tipple said, raising an eyebrow and dropping Mr Tipple's hand. Beatrice stared at the twins intently while they twiddled with their fingers and toes.

'We've had numerous complaints from parents. Is it correct you attend Chumsworth?' PC Dilks asked the twins.

'Yes,' they said, gulping.

'Mrs Tipple, I'm afraid your daughters are being accused of breaking into other people's homes in the middle of the night and appearing in other children's bedrooms… other children from their school.'

It all made sense to the twins now – the girl in the toilet. But why? How?

'That's insane,' Mr Tipple said, grabbing the arm of his chair tightly.

'I'm afraid not, Mr Tipple. We've got quite a backlog of complaints, starting from October. It seems your girls have been appearing in children's bedrooms and asking them to sign a book for them. To join some sort of gang, for children to sign themselves over to them. It's quite disturbing actually.'

'What utter nonsense. My girls are tucked up safe in their beds all night. How dare you come in here telling me otherwise!'

'Mrs Tipple, I would like to point out to you that your daughters are currently learning about the witches of Salem at school… and it's looking very likely at this time that they're imitating the behaviour they're learning about.'

'Rubbish. Do you not think you should be paying attention to something of more importance? Like my other daughter? Like… Caitlyn?'

'Mrs Tipple, I know this is a very sad time for you and your family, and we are doing our best to find her, but I need to make you aware of the fact that we're going to have to make your daughters suspects in this case. They're showing signs that appear to be the same as this "black figure" everyone's talking about. Your daughters may think it funny appearing in rooms and trying to recreate the past, but they're putting themselves at great risk. It certainly doesn't help that they were the last to be with Caitlyn before she disappeared.'

'I was there too!' Mrs Tipple said, jumping up out of her chair and grabbing her hair. 'I saw that black... *thing* standing before her... I saw the light flashing in front of my eyes when it took her. My other daughters were crying, screaming for help. Does it not occur to you that that *thing* tried to take Jenna and Jessica as well?'

'Please, Mrs Tipple, if you could just...' PC Dilks said, until something stopped him midway. With a terrified face, PC Dilks looked out of the window. 'Why... what in the...?' he said, pointing outside.

Jenna and Jessica and the rest of the family looked out the window and saw a black figure standing there watching them. Two seconds later it had gone.

Before the twins knew it, Boo had come downstairs and was rushing around the living room screaming, 'Help us! Help us all!'

Shocked at what he had seen, PC Dilks jumped up and down on the spot pointing at Boo. Mr and Mrs Tipple tried catching Boo to calm him down, but were unsuccessful and they ended up crashing into the Christmas tree, knocking it to the ground.

With Boo still bouncing around the house and the rest of the Tipples trying to calm him down, Beatrice stood in the corner of the room and slowly got out her mobile phone.

'Beatrice, don't you dare start filming!' Uncle Patrick squealed. Put your phone *down*!' But Beatrice carried on filming what was unravelling in the living room. Before the twins knew it, all of the Christmas decorations came crashing down.

'Boo, calm down!' the twins screamed. But Boo didn't listen as he whirled around the living room even faster now, still shouting, 'Help us! Help us all!'

Ignoring Boo's moment of panic, Uncle Patrick leaped over to where Beatrice was standing, his hands reaching out in front of him. 'Don't you dare upload that to social media, Beatrice! Don't you dare!' But it was too late. The video was loading by the time Uncle Patrick snatched her phone off her. 'Why, you little! How can I stop…? Blasted social media!'

Moments later, Jenna and Jessica heard the front door go, causing the family to pause. But not PC Dilks, as he was making his way out of the living room to check upstairs. When Mr and Mrs Tipple ran after him, Jenna and Jessica saw a bright flash of light in the hallway.

'Nooo!' Mrs Tipple screamed. Mr Tipple blocked his eyes from the bright light and nearly fell down the stairs. It was the black figure, and the black figure seemed to have taken PC Dilks.

Aunt Maud and Uncle Patrick had other considerations as to what was actually happening in the Tipple house on Bacton Square (besides Beatrice's video upload), and they were grabbing the PlayStation and all the other electrical goods they had sent to the house and were throwing them in the bin. Aunt Maud was flustered and began shouting at Mrs Tipple, who was now in the living room and was nearly as pale as Boo.

'You can't invite the police in here!' Aunt Maud screamed as she grabbed a set of Beats earphones and charged towards the kitchen. She then pointed at all the remaining goods spread around the house that she and Patrick had sent and said, 'That's stolen, that's stolen, that's stolen!' and this continued until she'd pointed at every single item she had given the Tipples over the last few months. 'Apart from Oliver, he's legit,' Aunt Maud said, catching her breath and smiling at Uncle Patrick proudly.

'We haven't got time to worry about your petty crimes, Maud!' Mrs Tipple screamed, causing pictures and mirrors to fall from the walls. 'We have to sort this mess out! My babies are in the frame for what happened to Caitlyn! This can't be happening! This isn't happening! This isn't happening! This *isn't* HAPPENING!'

'Oh shut up!' Maud shouted, and she slapped Mrs Tipple around the face. 'This *is* happening. And you need to deal with it.'

This wasn't good. It was not good at all, because now they knew the twins were the number one suspects. And the fact they were now the last to be seen with Dilks too just made it worse.

It was midnight by the time Mrs Tipple had told the house that the story is this… they hadn't seen PC Dilks that night. They hadn't seen him at all. PC Dilks may have intended to come here, but clearly he didn't even make it to the front door.

Mr and Mrs Tipple, Uncle Patrick and the twins spent the rest of the night putting the tree back up and cleaning up the rest of the mess Boo had created.

'You need to delete that video, Beatrice,' Patrick said as he picked up some broken baubles.

'I don't know what you're talking about,' Beatrice said sharply, picking up some tinsel.

'Don't play dumb with me, Beatrice!'

'I'm not!'

'God help me I'll make sure there will be no more help when it comes to your weight! You will delete that video at once.' said Uncle Patrick, wagging a finger.

'But it's got five hundred views and counting.'

'I don't care if it's viewed by the queen!'

'I want to see if it gets shares,' said Beatrice huffily.

'Shares? You want that thing to get shares! For goodness' sake, Beatrice! Delete it *now*!'

'I won't!'

'DELETE IT!' they all barked at once, which caused Beatrice to storm off upstairs as she deleted the video.

'It had five hundred views and *count-ing*!' she said as she wept as she thumped up the stairs.

Aunt Maud then came in from the kitchen holding a plate of biscuits and an iPhone. 'Well, I suppose we can keep this one, can't we?' she said, faking a smile. 'Well that's settled then. We'll keep just the phone… and maybe the telly… well, all right then, and the PlayStation too. Can't leave that one out, can we?'

Aunt Maud said before placing the phone on the table. She then brushed herself down as if she was starting a new day and held up the plate in the other hand. 'Biccy anyone?'

CHAPTER NINE

*

THE PAINTING

It was next morning when the twins awoke startled and sweaty. It was probably a nightmare they'd had, but if it was, they couldn't remember it.

They could hear Boo snoring under Jessica's bed and quickly put their dressing gowns on before going downstairs. They were expecting a knock on the door at any moment due to PC Dilks' disappearance, and it made them nervous, causing Jessica's voice to squeak when she was spoken to.

As they entered the living room, Aunt Maud and Uncle Patrick were sitting on the sofas sulking.

'Don't talk to them,' Mrs Tipple snapped. 'They've just had a telling off about the stolen goods they had delivered here. Come to think of it,' she said as she tottered off to the kitchen suddenly locking the kitchen door, 'you two need to get on with your homework. We can't let things slip now. If your grades go down, it will look even more suspicious. I'm sorry. I know it's not nice. But we really need to clamp down on all this odd activity. Even Oliver is being locked in the kitchen until he knows how to stop hanging around with teenagers and wearing our clothes.' She paused and sighed before continuing. 'He even made an appearance at the pub the other night and came home drunk. I found him sleeping in the bushes outside.'

Jenna and Jessica went back upstairs to their bedrooms and opened their books. Their homework was to research the witches of Salem, and so they did.

With Boo now awake, they looked at paintings of the Salem witch trials together. Huddled on the same bed, they saw pictures of crowds swarming around the accused witches. They then went on to read underneath one of the paintings about one of the women, who was known by the name Martha Carrier and was accused of being a witch.

She was an unpopular woman who had little money. She also had her first child out of wedlock. Rumour had it she had spread smallpox and had spoken sharply to her neighbours.

'Women who had had a child before marriage were frowned upon in those days. And for that reason alone, it is probably the reason she has been accused of being a witch' read a quote in one of the books.

A little further down the page was a script from the trial itself. It said that one of the victims of Martha's magic, someone called Susannah, cried out telling the court she could see an evil man dressed in black and that he may be the devil himself. She told the court he appeared a few times and was called 'the black man'.

They then learned that Martha Carrier continued to plead her innocence and was later given the death sentence.

As Jenna and Jessica continued reading, they felt they could relate to the accused woman, because they had also been accused of things they hadn't done.

The moment passed quickly and they continued flicking through the pages, until they came across something rather unexpected. To their shock, they saw a woman who looked like Miss Snippings. This woman was standing in front of a crowd waiting to be executed. Could it be? Jenna studied it at length and Jessica took it from under her nose now and then to study it herself, and eventually they were both fighting over it and not studying it at all.

'I had it first,' stated Jenna, ripping the book from Jessica's hands.

'But you're not sharing it,' said Jessica, snatching it back.

Jenna blew air into Jessica's face. She knew this bothered Jessica more than a slap might because it bothered *her* as well. Blowing and breathing on one another was far more intrusive. Jessica blew back and they spent about a minute and a half blowing and breathing on each other, completely forgetting about the book, until they looked up and saw Boo waving it at them above their beds.

'Give us the book,' they pleaded.

'I'm going to hold it for you both,' said Boo. Jenna

and Jessica didn't argue. They stared back at the picture. This woman had ginger hair like Miss Snippings and a crooked posture like Miss Snippings. There was nothing about this picture to suggest it wasn't Miss Snippings other than the dates, for no person could ever live for that long. Could she be a witch from Salem? No, possibly not. But they couldn't help but feel they would be wrong to dismiss it.

At that instant they rushed down the stairs to ask if they could phone Tommy. They walked towards the living room and peered inside. Their mum was spying out of the window.

'You ask,' Jenna whispered to Jessica.

'No, you ask. Mum will listen to you more…'

'Girls, what is it?' Mrs Tipple said, jerking her head around.

'Well… we were just wondering if—'

'Come on, quickly, spit it out, you two. I'm on police watch.'

'Well, we just wanted to ask if we could phone Tommy… about homework,' Jenna said uncomfortably.

'Oh all right then,' she said firmly, not taking her eyes off Bacton Square.

Jenna and Jessica hurried upstairs and grabbed for the phone in their bedroom. Surprised at how easy the conversation had gone, they stood holding the phone between both of them and whispered as loudly as they could, firstly filling Tommy in about the black figure coming to their home and snatching P.C Dilks, and how they are in the firing line for their missing sister, causing

Tommy to spill off a load of 'oh my god's' and 'well I never's' and then finally telling Tommy to look at the painting of Miss Snippings in *his* copy of the book, which he did.

'Well I never,' Tommy said, breathing heavily. 'I bet she's a ghost!'

'What are we going to do, Tommy?'

'I dunno. Shall we try touching her when we see her next? I bet our hands go straight through her...'

'I'm not touching her. You can but I won't. Besides, she managed to throw us in the hole of black with no problem,' said Jenna.

'I'll tell you what we need to do. We need to find room thirteen. There's a reason no one's allowed in there,' said Tommy.

'But how are we going to do that if nobody knows where it is?'

'Rubbish. Of course someone knows where it is, and that has to be the witch herself.'

'We can't just ask her where it is. She'll put us in the hole of black again,' moaned Jessica.

Silence hung over them while all three thought intently. They didn't know what it was they were looking for exactly, but any sort of answer or clue had to be better than none. They needed to know exactly what Miss Snippings was, and room thirteen was a better place to start than any other.

'Ah, I know!' Tommy shouted. 'We'll sneak into her office, first day back at school. If there are keys in there, we'll put them in every door till one fits.'

'We *can't* do that. We'll get caught! And how are we going to know it's the *right* key?' said Jessica.

'Well, we'll just guess!' Tommy snapped. 'I have to go, my mum's calling me. She's taking me out to see some Christmas lights and then we're going shopping for sweets. I'll see you in school first day back. Be there half an hour before school starts… meet me outside the gates.'

'Okay, have a good Christmas.'

'Okay, and you.'

The phone went dead and the girls finished their homework as quickly as they could.

*

Next morning they woke up again in a sweat. This time Jessica more so than her sister.

'My God, you look rough,' Jenna said to Jessica as they got dressed together, only this time Jessica seemed to be slower than Jenna. And Jessica seemed to be slower all day. She even ate her dinner slower, until she gave up and asked if she had to have any of it at all.

'What's wrong with you, Jessica?' Mrs Tipple said, taking her plate away from the table.

'I'll have it,' Beatrice said, seizing the plate from her mum's hands.

'I hope you're not coming down with anything,' her mum said, before turning to her dad. 'Do you think she's all right?' she whispered to him as she began washing up. Mr Tipple shrugged and said he was taking Oliver out on the lead.

'Good luck!' Aunt Maud shouted with a mouth full of

potatoes. 'Last time I did that he howled so loudly it blew my skirt up.'

By the time it was night-time, Jessica was so exhausted she had gone to bed before Jenna had even started getting ready for it. The light was already out and Jessica was fast asleep as Jenna crept into her own bed. When she pulled the cover over herself and lay on her pillow, she could have sworn she saw something that wasn't Boo sleeping under Jessica's bed – a woman. And when she looked harder, that *woman* looked like Miss Snippings. Jenna blinked and focused on what she thought she saw, but this time when she looked it was nothing but Boo. Curled up. Fast asleep.

CHAPTER TEN

*

MISS SNIPPINGS' CLIPPINGS

It was after the Christmas holiday, early in the morning and Chumsworth's grounds were covered in ice. The twins met Tommy outside the school gates as planned and Jenna and Jessica couldn't help but feel it was nice to finally get away from the house, what with their mum being on police guard twenty-four seven. Although what lay ahead of them wasn't any better – just the thought of Miss Snippings catching them sneaking about made Jenna and Jessica shudder.

'So, what excuse did you give your mum then? Ya know… to get here early 'n' that?' Tommy said with a mouthful of bubblegum.

'We told Mum we didn't want to be at home at the moment,' Jessica said before they swept into the school grounds and hurried into the deserted reception area.

'And what do *you three* think you are doing here at this time?' It was Mr Smith.

'We, err… we find out what parts we have for the school production today, don't we?' said Tommy. 'We got here early to have a look.'

Mr Smith raised an eyebrow before speaking. 'Wait here one moment… I'll go and get the list,' he said, before pacing down the corridor until they could no longer see him.

'Quick,' Jenna said, and they all pressed their ears up against Miss Snippings' office. They didn't have any time to lose, not with Mr Smith hovering about.

'I can't hear a thing,' said Jenna.

'That means nothing,' Tommy interrupted. 'Ghosts don't really make noises.'

'Some might,'

'Okay, if that's what we are all going by, why don't we just barge in there right now?' Jessica said.

'Okay then,' said Tommy stubbornly.

'So we're just going to barge in there, are we?' asked Jessica.

'Yep.'

'Well go on then, Tommy,' urged Jessica.

'You first.'

'Oh, I'll do it!' Jenna said before grabbing the door by the handle. She went inside, with Jessica and Tommy following quickly. It wasn't long before they heard footsteps coming down the corridor.

'Quick! It's Mrs Greenose!' Tommy said, shutting the door. 'That was close.'

The three of them studied the office before getting to work. The room was filled with dark wooden furniture, which consisted of a desk, a cabinet, a bookshelf and a wardrobe. There was emerald-green carpet covering the floor and a mirror hanging on the wall.

'I'll do the desk,' Tommy insisted. 'One of you look inside the cabinet... the other keep an eye out.'

They worked their way through the drawers as quickly as they could. Tommy found a red book on top of the desk, and it seemed odd that it had no title and the pages he managed to flick through were blank. 'Weird,' he said as he tossed it aside.

'Oi, shall we plant something in here? Like needles on her chair?' he said, carrying on sifting through more paperwork and forgetting about the red book.

'No,' said Jessica, who had her eye stuck to the keyhole.

'Lock her out then... squatters' rights...'

'Definitely not, Tommy,' said Jenna, taking a load of papers from the cabinet and accidently dropping them on the floor. 'Help me, quick!' she said to Tommy, who was already rushing over to pick up the mess.

'All right, start an argument, tell her how you feel.'

'As if,' said Jessica.

'I might...' said Jenna.

'No you wouldn't,' said Jessica back.

'I agree with Jessica... you wouldn't say anything.'

'I said I might,' mumbled Jenna, who was rifling through the papers so fast her face was turning pink.

'Oh my word,' Tommy said, as he read one of the papers, which appeared to be an article about twins that had gone missing.

As Jenna picked up the rest, she too was holding a

handful of articles about missing twins. 'What's all this?' Jenna asked, sifting through them one by one.

Jessica looked round to see what all the fuss was about and nearly choked on her own spit when she saw what Jenna and Tommy were holding. When she turned back to spy through the keyhole, she gasped and ran towards Jenna and Tommy, helping them with the mess on the floor. 'Quick!' she said, 'Miss Snippings is coming!'

All at once, the three of them shoved the rest of the papers back in the drawers. Jenna, who was still holding some, was turning back and forth. She couldn't make up her mind as to whether she should make a run for it or put the papers away.

Tommy intervened and snatched them from Jenna to put them away before the three of them grabbed their bags and jumped into the wardrobe.

Patiently sitting in the dark, they heard the door handle creaking. A small glimpse of daylight crept in through the gap of the wardrobe door, which was useful to Tommy as he could carefully spy through it.

Miss Snippings walked in, closing the door behind her. She sat down stiffly at her desk and got out some paperwork. Typing away at her computer, Miss Snippings seemed to be turning her head every now and then in the direction of the cabinet. Something wasn't quite right and that something was a bit of paper sticking out of one of the drawers.

Miss Snippings stood up, moved over to the cabinet, put the bit of paper back in its place and pushed the drawer shut. Tommy moved away from the gap in the wardrobe door and Jenna and Jessica held their breaths.

Eventually feeling brave again, Tommy put his eye against the gap one last time, only to see something he didn't expect. He could no longer see the office, but there was an eye looking right back at him. One of Miss Snippings' grey eyes.

Tommy edged back quickly, careful not to make any noise. Taking it upon herself to have a look, Jenna couldn't see the eye but instead she could see the figure of Miss Snippings standing by the bookshelf with her back facing them.

'If you three would like to leave now,' said Miss Snippings.

Shocked, the twins froze and didn't reply.

'I said… if you could all *leave now*,' said Miss Snippings again.

Beside themselves with horror, Jenna and Jessica faced Tommy. 'We have to go,' whispered Jessica.

'What? Not with *her* there,' whispered Tommy back.

'We have to. She's told us to. She knows we're in here,' said Jenna frantically.

'Are you mad? I've not heard her say anything,' whispered Tommy again.

'She's told us to leave twice. How are you not hearing her?' asked Jessica quietly.

'I think we should go then,' said Tommy.

'What about squatters' rights?' said Jenna sarcastically, but before Tommy could answer, Jenna and Jessica were already stumbling out of the wardrobe.

'My God, this is *crazy*,' said Tommy, following them out.

They crawled across the floor slowly with Tommy taking the lead.

With Miss Snippings still standing by the bookshelf, they managed to get to the door before Jessica screamed and stood up stiffly with an arched back.

'It hurts! I can feel needles and pins!' she cried, as Jenna and Tommy rushed to her rescue. They pulled at her arms as Jessica cried and cried. 'Needles and pins! Needles and pins!' she wailed. 'It's Miss Snippings. She's torturing me! She's torturing me!'

When Jenna and Tommy looked at Miss Snippings, she was still standing in the same position as when they'd last looked: by the bookshelf, with her back turned to them. Tommy and Jenna dragged Jessica out of Miss Snippings' office and closed the door behind them.

They reached the corridor in a panic, and it was now buzzing with other pupils rushing to their lessons. They turned towards their classroom, heads down, and hid behind a group of children who were going in the same direction as them and rushed to safety.

'Quick, in room one,' said Tommy, holding onto a distraught Jessica. Jenna and Tommy fell through the door of room one and dumped Jessica to the floor. 'We can sort ourselves out in here before we go to class. Mr Smith can't know what's happened. He won't believe us,' gasped Tommy.

'Are you all right?' said Jenna, bending down to Jessica.

'I feel okay now,' she said in a sweaty state. 'But look… it's the scratches on the door you were talking about,

Tommy. The three scratches on the locked door inside room one.'

'Yeah, I know, but we can't worry about that now. We have to get to class,' said Tommy, before the three of them eventually made their way to their lesson.

'And where have *you three* been?' Mr Smith asked abruptly when they walked in. The three of them paused on the spot until Tommy had an answer of his own.

'Well where were *you*, sir? We were waiting in the corridor for ages and you didn't show up.'

CHAPTER ELEVEN

*

ROOM THIRTEEN, PART ONE

Tommy hung around the classroom door at break time while Jenna and Jessica asked Mr Smith for a copy of the list of parts for the school production, careful to not look too suspicious following their actions earlier that morning. Pretending to study the parts with interest, Jenna and Jessica moved towards the door slowly, not noticing that Tommy had worked himself up over something.

'You'll never guess what,' Tommy squealed, barely containing his excitement. But Jenna and Jessica had noticed something of their own.

'Tommy, shhh… listen, me and Jessica have just seen our parts for the All School Production, and we're all "runners". Do you *know* what that means? We have no part in the play. No part at all. Just skivvies doing whatever anyone wants us to.'

'And Ruby's got the part of a witch. She gets to stand centre stage and even gets to say some lines,' said Jessica as they made their way outside to the playground.

'You two, you're not listening,' said Tommy urgently.

'And did you *hear* the way Miss Snippings spoke to us when we were stuck in that office… in her *cave*,' added Jenna.

'I didn't hear Miss Snippings talking, but we'll work that one out later. What I'm trying to tell you now is *I think I know where room thirteen is*!' Tommy barked impatiently.

'What? Where? How?' said Jessica, leaning in towards him.

'Well, when we were in room one earlier… when Jessica pointed out the three scratches on the door inside. Come on, work it out… Room one… that's the number one and there are *three* scratches on the inside of the door… that's the number three… I think that's room thirteen. So really, there's not actually a room thirteen, which is why nobody knows where it is. Are you getting this?' Tommy said, and he was looking at Jessica, who seemed to have come over all funny, like she was trying to stay awake, like she wanted to go to sleep.

'Jessica… Jessica… JESSICA!' Both Tommy and Jenna screamed to wake her up.

'Yes, I heard you… room thirteen… inside room one. Is that why you were throwing rubbers at us in maths?'

'Yes!'

'Tommy, are you sure?' Jenna said, now supporting Jessica with her arm.

'Not completely, but it's the only answer that makes sense. Jessica, are you sure you're okay? You look a bit… well a bit off.'

*

The next morning at Chumsworth, Jenna, Jessica and Tommy all met outside the hall with the rest of the school. It was the first day of rehearsals and they had just picked up their 'Runners' T-shirts, which were big black baggy things that drowned them.

Soon enough, the hall was packed, leaving only enough room for Miss Snippings to enter, and when she did she gave Jenna, Jessica and Tommy some nasty looks.

'Ignore her,' Tommy whispered. 'She's just playing mind games with us.' But Jenna and Jessica found that hard to believe, especially when they saw the ghostlike blackbirds that had originally been sitting on the roof of Chumsworth slowly building in number outside the windows of the hall.

'She knows we were in there, Tommy, in her office. She spoke to us and told us to get out. But she must have done it in a way so that you didn't hear anything. She must have done it telepathically!'

'See, you know why that is, don't you? It's because *she's a ghost*. Well, I'm not putting up with it. If she carries on playing games I'm not gonna do what anyone tells me to do.'

'I don't think I feel too good,' said Jessica faintly.

'Don't act weak now, Jessica. That's just what she wants us to do! And now we know where room thirteen is… well, we need to get back in there, don't we.'

'I can't help it. Whenever I think of *her* I go all funny.'

'I'm getting sick of this. That's it!' said Tommy, slamming down his bag. 'I'm not doing any work today,' he said aggressively before Miss Snippings took the stage. 'And I don't see why you two should either.'

'Good morning, children!' Miss Snippings said, and everyone went silent. She paused for a moment of glory before speaking again. 'And now…'

'Oh, shut up,' muttered Tommy under his breath, causing the rest of the school to instantly turn their attention to him.

'Did somebody say something?' Miss Snippings barked. 'I take it somebody's feeling brave this morning… very *brave*. Can that person please come forward!'

'It was me,' said Tommy, inching forward. Jenna and Jessica could see he was flustered, but it wasn't an embarrassed flustered. It was an angry flustered.

'Ah, Tommy Grinch. I should have known. And what is it, *Tommy*? What was it you wanted to say?' sneered Miss Snippings, who was now so tense she was almost quivering.

'I said… SHUT UP!'

Gasps spread across the hall and a stunned Miss Snippings stood motionless. Feeling sick to the pits of their stomachs, Jenna and Jessica couldn't think of a way out of this one.

Miss Snippings stood still for a few moments more before letting out a rancid laugh. It was the sort of laugh that felt like it was travelling through every corner of your brain and back out of your nose.

'If everyone could kindly leave right now,' said Miss Snippings through gritted teeth, faking a smile.

It wasn't every day the pupils of Chumsworth didn't immediately do as they were told when directed to by Miss Snippings, but today was one of those days. Everybody in the hall stood in anticipation before Miss Snippings really lost her patience.

'Everyone get out! GET OUT! Except for you, Grinch. And your twinny little friends!'

As the children and teachers rushed out, they were ordered to not look at Jenna, Jessica or Tommy. 'Keep your heads down. Eyes shut!'

And they did just that.

It took what felt like a whole age before the hall was cleared, but when it was, Jenna and Jessica didn't look forward to what was ahead of them. Tommy was signalling to them, glancing towards Miss Snippings' waist. They didn't realise what was going on at first but finally they saw a set of keys dangling from a belt. They didn't know for sure which keys they were, but they could take a good guess.

'So you think you can tell me to shut up, do you?' Miss Snippings said as she moved her deformed figure down the steps and off the stage until she was face-to-face with Jenna, Jessica and Tommy. 'Well, let's see how clever you think you are when you haven't got an audience, Mr Grinch.'

'I don't need no audience, Miss,' Tommy said, taking at least two steps forward. 'And I'm not the one pretending to be something I'm not.'

'Maybe not you, Tommy, but what about your friends? Are you sure they're everything *you think* they are?'

'I know *exactly* who they are.'

'Is that so? Jenna, Jessica, why don't you point at something… just once.'

Tommy looked baffled as he turned to look at them. Jenna and Jessica could see more ghostlike birds arriving outside the windows of the hall. Some were flapping their wings, others were perched as if made from stone.

'No, it's okay, Miss,' Jessica said weakly, not knowing what to look at, bird or Snippings, bird or Snippings…

'It wasn't a question. It was an *order*!'

'And they said *NO*!' Tommy said, before charging straight for her. Tommy barged straight into Miss Snippings, grabbing the set of keys from her waist.

'Catch!' Tommy yelled, throwing the keys into the air, and the twins caught them unsteadily. 'Run! To room thirteen! Come on!'

'B-b-but, Tommy!'

'COME ON!'

The twins and Tommy ran as fast their legs could carry them towards the doors of the hall, on the way to room thirteen.

CHAPTER TWELVE

*

ROOM THIRTEEN, PART TWO

Jenna and Jessica didn't mean to shatter the glass windows surrounding the hall (causing the blackbirds to enter the school and chase them) as they made their escape to room thirteen, nor did they mean to knock every pupil up into the air when they bellowed to them to get out of the way. The situation had got out of control, as had their magic moods. Miss Snippings had tried shutting the hall doors with power of her own, but the twins magic overruled it and swung the doors back to release them.

Running down the corridors with a flock of birds behind them, they eventually reached room thirteen, shutting the doors behind them with their minds. And when they did, they heard the bird's beaks slamming into the wood of the door. Jenna and Jessica then fumbled with the keys and had the horrid task of choosing which key was the right one.

'Just think, if you were Miss Snippings, which one would you choose?' enquired Tommy.

'Black!' the twins said at once. 'The black one!' And they put it in, but before they could turn it, Tommy stopped them.

'Wait! Before we go in, are you two ready? I mean really ready? We don't know what we're going to find in there. What if she's the black figure? What if she's the *twin snatcher*?'

'Then we'll save them,' Jessica said. 'But wait, what if Caitlyn's in there?'

'Then let's go in!' Jenna shouted

'But what if she's... what if she's not moving,' Jessica said uncomfortably.

Jenna and Jessica stared at each other in deep thought before Tommy encouraged them. 'Then you two are going to get her out and bring her home, no matter what condition she's in, because she's your sister! Now TURN... THAT... KEY!'

Jenna and Jessica turned the key, and as the door opened there was a blast of wind and then a stampede of twins came rushing out into the corridors of Chumsworth, letting in the flock of ghostlike birds. The twins and Tommy dashed inside, frantically weaving in and out of the twins who were heading in the opposite direction to them.

Jessica grabbed a girl who was slightly taller than her and had the same honey-coloured hair as their sister Caitlyn. 'Caitlyn, I've got you!' screamed Jessica, only to be confronted by someone who wasn't Caitlyn at all, just another twin running for their life. Jessica let go at once and carried on through the crowd and down a long corridor made of stone with Jenna and Tommy until they found themselves deep underground, surrounded by more dark walls made of stone. The ghostlike blackbirds had failed to get that far, and considering the twins and Tommy had done nothing to stop them themselves, they wondered if they were under some sort of order from Miss Snippings.

They eventually came to a halt as they reached a dead end. It didn't take long for them to realise they were in a room full of blankets, which they guessed were for the beds for all the twins.

'Has anyone seen her? Has anyone seen Caitlyn?' asked Jenna.

'Well I haven't,' said Tommy, bending over, trying to catch his breath.

'No, neither have I,' admitted Jessica glumly.

'Caitlyn!' screamed Jenna at the top of her lungs.

'Caitlyn! Come out! It's us! Jenna and Jessica!' Jessica shouted desperately.

But Caitlyn didn't show.

To Jenna's and Jessica's disgust, Miss Snippings did.

'Well, well, well, haven't we got ourselves into a mess,' Miss Snippings said, appearing from the dark at the far end of the room.

'This is a mess, yes... but it's *your* mess!' Jessica shouted, but she quickly wished she hadn't, because who knew what Miss Snippings was capable of doing to them now.

'Actually, it's *our* mess,' Miss Snippings corrected.

'And how do you work that one out, eh?' said Tommy bravely.

'Well, let's look at the facts, shall we?' said Miss Snippings, focusing on the twins. 'Did PC Dilks turn up to your house? Did he accuse you of being the number one suspects in Caitlyn's case? Are you down as harassing children from this school?'

'That means nothing! We've just found all the missing twins! You're the black figure! We've solved the case!' screamed Jenna a little enthusiastically. Not only was she answering back with confidence, but the twins seemed to be in with a chance of *winning*. Had Jenna turned a page?

'You've solved nothing! All you've done is release a load of twins! For all the police know, you were in on it and decided for whatever reason to let them go.'

Jenna looked down at her feet and began working out what to say next, and Jessica looked just as puzzled and worried as her sister. Finally, Jenna plucked up the courage to answer back.

'That's not going to work. How are young children like us going to be able to get all those twins in here?'

'Well, because of your *gift*.'

'Gift?' Tommy said.

'Yes... *gift*.'

'Tommy, we—' Jenna went to explain but was interrupted.

'It appears to me that your friends aren't as honest as you think they are, Tommy. Your friends have magical abilities and they can't even tell you that.'

'Is it true? Are you really magical?' said Tommy, shocked.

'Yes,' answered Jenna, looking to the ground.

'So you can do things other people can't?'

'Yes.'

'You can make things appear and disappear?'

'Yes.'

'Like sweets… and money?'

'Yes.'

'That's awesome! I don't care what you are. You're my friends, and friends stick together! Magic or not!' said Tommy, but suddenly he stopped when Miss Snippings edged a little closer.

'Oh, but what a shame it is,' she sneered, 'because now the whole world will know all about it.'

'How do you work that one out?' snapped Jessica, edging back slightly from Miss Snippings, who was coming closer still.

'Well… you've just shown the entire school what you can do. I saw you lifting kids into the air when you shouted, though it does make me laugh that you call it a gift. Why, you're nothing but a pair of witches.'

'Witches?' Jenna and Jessica asked.

'Yes… *witches*. Don't you know about our history? I've been trying to teach it to you in school. About the Salem witch trials. Notice the similarities? The animals that appeared… the birds? And all gifted people, as you put it, got killed!'

'No, that's wrong! We were made to dance in the air!' argued Jessica, which caused Miss Snippings to let out thunderous laughter.

'And what do you think being "made to dance in the air" is? It's being hung, that's what it is!' Miss Snippings said, as if with great pleasure.

'You're lying!' bellowed the twins together.

'No, no, I'm not. Go home and ask your mum and dad... I *dare* you.'

'She'll just tell us the story of the floating woman! The one where—'

'I know that story, Jessica! I'm the floating woman! It was me that was caught! It was me that was made to dance in the air because I got hung! Why do you think I have to wear this scarf around my neck?' Miss Snippings shrieked before whipping off the scarf and revealing a scar behind it. 'And it was my twin that sat right back and let it happen! That's why I hate twins!'

'Because you died and she didn't?' asked a puzzled Jenna.

'No, because she watched me die and did nothing about it! I see all these other twins having a bond... this *special* bond everybody talks about. Why did't we have that? And it makes me sick to watch it. And then you and your sister go and make it worse, because not only do you two have a special bond, but it appears that you also have one with your older sister... Caitlyn!'

'Where is she? What have you done with her?' Jenna demanded, but Miss Snippings was too wrapped up in her own tantrum to listen.

'Stupid Caitlyn went and saved you. Stupid Caitlyn put herself in the firing line to save you both. Stupid Caitlyn this, stupid Caitlyn that! I went to your house at night to get *you two*! But you both went and woke up your big sister because you were scared of the noises outside… and what does Caitlyn do? When all three of you decide to sneak outside to see what all the fuss was about, Caitlyn knew the minute she saw me and ran straight towards me to save you both! Do you remember her crying out, telling you both to run?'

'Well, yes, but…' said Jenna and Jessica together, now wiping tears from their eyes.

'And do you know what really got on my wick?' Miss Snippings snapped further. 'Your *stupid* letters to Father Christmas… Dear Father Christmas, please can you bring back our sister, Caitlyn. We promise to be good and won't argue with her any more… Dear Father Christmas, even though you couldn't bring Caitlyn home last year, we still think you might be able to this year. We promise to be extra, extra good and might be allowed to give you an extra mince pie. We won't even ask for presents this year, just our sister—'

'Where *is* she!' shrieked Jessica. She no longer cared what Miss Snippings might do. Jessica was losing control. She was no longer bottling it up, hiding.

'Oh, for God's sake! She's not *here*! She's not anywhere! Caitlyn no longer exists!'

'What are you saying?' said Jenna, holding back the tears.

'I killed her!'

'How can you do this to us?' Jenna and Jessica shouted, now sobbing into their runner's T-shirts.

'Quite easily actually. Just as I haunted you in the school. That presence you felt – that was… me,' said Miss

Snippings, raising her finger proudly. 'Me appearing as you in the corridor when that girl collapsed and said it was you two… That was me too… Turning up in other pupils' bedrooms, also appearing as you both… Do you see where this is going? I couldn't snatch you because your sister saved you, but I could torment you both. Been feeling a bit peculiar recently, Jessica? I've been trying to make you feel unwell so you can't do twinny little things together, like going to bed at the same time, getting dressed at the same time, and it started to work until…' Miss Snippings shot an evil look at Tommy, who was edging towards a pile of stones. 'Until this one!' Miss Snippings threw Tommy into the air and whacked him against a wall. 'Until this one threw a hissy fit and actually stood up to me! And what can I say? Now we are here.'

'Tommy! Are you all right?' the twins shouted, rushing to his rescue.

'I'm f-fine,' Tommy said, plucking up the strength to stand up. 'Face it, Miss Snippings! You've been caught. You won't get away with it. We won't let you!' he said, barely able to stand.

'Let's see about that, shall we! I'll take everything you own! I'll ruin you all!' Miss Snippings said, clapping her hands together and causing the stone walls around them to crumble and crash…

*

Meanwhile, in the Tipple house, Aunt Maud was telling Mrs Tipple about how she could change her appearance to look like PC Dilks and pretend she was him at work. 'I'll just trot into the station and be him. No one will even question it… and who knows… I might get some inside gossip about Caitlyn's case.' It was at that moment when the walls of the Tipple house began caving in as well.

'What in the…' Mrs Tipple said. 'Maud, if this is your way of transforming this house into a mansion, stop! Stop it at once!'

'But I'm not doing anything!'

'Well where's Patrick? It must be him then.'

'Patrick!' they both screamed

'I'm on the toilet!' wailed Patrick from upstairs.

'See, he's on the toilet. It's got nothing to do with us!'

'Maud!' Patrick shouted from the toilet. 'Maud, stop it, will you! You said you weren't going to transform the house until we were out of the doghouse about the stolen goods.'

'Maud, if this is you I'm going to kill you,' Mrs Tipple said, now holding onto the wall of the kitchen as the house wobbled violently. Aunt Maud, saying nothing, held onto Mrs Tipple with one arm and clutched Oliver under the other.

'We're under attack! We're under attack!' said Boo, as he came fleeing in, dodging bits of brick and dust that were falling from the ceiling.

The birds that surrounded the Tipple house took off from the roof and the steps and headed towards Chumsworth.

*

Miss Snippings cackled as she watched Jenna, Jessica and Tommy dodging stones that fell from above. Weaving in and out of plenty of near misses, it wasn't their only problem. Miss Snippings was now creating what looked like bolts of lightning aimed at Jenna, Jessica and Tommy.

'Do something!' Tommy yelled, and Jenna and Jessica realised they had no choice but to use the force they'd tried so long to tame and hide. They each pointed at Miss Snippings but only managed to create a few frogs.

'What are you two doing?' Tommy screeched.

'We can't control it! I think it's because we think she's *slimey*,' yelled Jenna while pulling a frog from her wrist.

'Exactly, Tommy, can't you see? She's… she's drenched in the stuff.'

'Well try harder,' said Tommy, diving out of the way of yet another attempt to be hit by Miss Snippings' magic.

It was at that moment that Jenna and Jessica, for the first time, used their magic accordingly and emitted something that wasn't like electricity but was more like a bolt of red fire. It struck Miss Snippings on her toes first, which were still dangling in the air, but when they went for a second hit, something was coming from behind them… the blackbirds from their home.

The blackbirds flooded in, followed by Miss Snippings' ghostly birds, and they covered her until Miss Snippings was nothing but a mass of birds, each of them pecking at her while the ghostlike ones tried to fight them off. There was only one bird that didn't join in the fight and that was the one that had tried to stop them leaving home on the first day they started Chumsworth, the one that took shelter in their room when Aunt Maud and Uncle Patrick dumped Beatrice at their home. It pecked at Jenna's and Jessica's shoulders, attacking them until they had no choice but to leave, but before they did, Jessica grabbed the bird and threw it across the room. They ran towards the exit of room thirteen and Chumsworth with Tommy. At any minute Chumsworth was going to collapse into nothing but a heap of rubble and the twins and Tommy had to get out.

As they made their escape back through the entrance of room thirteen, they didn't dare look to see Miss Snippings' fate, but they could hear the cries of the blackbirds that attacked her.

Finally breathing fresh air, they found themselves outside the building and they rushed to join the rest of the pupils on one of the playgrounds. The teachers and pupils were stunned with what they were witnessing, that the great Chumsworth was crumbling in front of them. Chumsworth's walls and emerald-green carpet were nothing more than a pile of dust and thick smoke. Moments later, blackbirds flew up from the remains of the building and flocked around the children in a protective manner. The ghostlike ones didn't reappear.

The twins that had been released earlier gazed around at the sight; some were children, some adults.

'You know what this means, don't you?' said Tommy, covered in dust from top to toe.

'What?' asked Jenna.

'Well, this gift you have… this thing you've hidden… it's all going to come out now. You do know that, don't you? All those people captured by Miss Snippings, they're probably going to know she had powers like you too.'

Jenna and Jessica didn't answer, but they did nearly make a run for it when a dusty and angry Mr Smith came over with PC Dilks.

Then, to the twins' pleasure, more police turned up and took the girls home… to what was left of it, anyway.

*

Aunt Maud answered the door sheepishly, still holding onto Oliver, who was covered in toilet roll and a helping of brick dust. The Tipple house had nearly no roof and with many of its windows broken.

With the twins safe and sound at home, the blackbirds huddled outside on the steps, with the only exception being the one that usually stayed in the house.

'No doubt we will be in touch with all of you,' said a policeman who was busy stepping over the birds that squawked around his feet. 'Until then, may I advise you not to talk to anybody about what happened today, and you'll need to start writing statements as soon as you find it possible.'

Aunt Maud nodded and closed the door hastily. With Uncle Patrick now stuck on the toilet and Mrs Tipple supporting a kitchen cupboard with an arm, it took at least two hours after Mr Tipple arrived home for them to start mending their house.

But of course that wasn't their only problem. Jenna and Jessica had the sad news to break to their mum and dad about Caitlyn being dead. Not to mention the fact they had used their magic in public. But now, with Miss Snippings gone, they could at least go to sleep at night not worrying about whether they were going to be snatched or not. But with Chumsworth destroyed, what were people going to think of them now? For who would have thought that such destruction could come from the Tipple twins and their gift.

Bibliography

Witch Hunt, by Marc Aronson
The Salem Witch Trials, by Marilyn K. Roach